GIRLS AROUND THE HOUSE

GIRLS AROUND THE HOUSE

M.A.C. Farrant

POLESTAR
BOOK PUBLISHERS

Polestar Book Publishers acknowledges the ongoing support of The Canada Council; the British Columbia Ministry of Small Business, Tourism and Culture through the BC Arts Council; and the Government of Canada through the Book Publishing Industry Development Program (BPIDP).

"Skidney" appeared in the May 20, 1999, issue of *Monday Magazine*, Victoria, BC. The phrase "You're Young, You're Dumb, And You're Wrong" is from the essay "Circling The Squires" by David R. Slavitt, which appeared in *Dumbing Down — Essays On The Strip Mining Of American Culture*, edited by Katharine Washburn and John Thornton (Norton 1996). "The Princess, the Queen & the Withered King" and "Tic-Tac-Doe" appeared in slightly different forms in *What's True, Darling* (Polestar, 1997).

Cover photograph by Andrea Lowe
Cover design by Val Speidel.
Author photo by Terry Farrant.
Printed and bound in Canada.

CANADIAN CATALOGUING IN PUBLICATION DATA
        Farrant, M.A.C. (Marion Alice Coburn)
        Girls around the house
        ISBN 1-896095-93-3
        I. Title.
        PS8561.A76G57 1999   C813'.54   C99-910735-6
        PR9199.3.F355G57 1999

Library of Congress Catalogue Number: 99-64173

Polestar Book Publishers
P.O. Box 5238, Station B
Victoria, British Columbia
Canada   V8R 6N4

In the United States:
Polestar Book Publishers
1436 West Randolph Street
Chicago, Illinois
USA   60607

Canadä

99 00 01 02 • 5 4 3 2 1

Enormous thanks to the girls around the house, Anna, Kristy and Sara, and the boys, Terry and Bill.

And to my editor, Lynn Henry; publisher Michelle Benjamin; and publicist Emiko Morita. Thanks also to Alma Lee for her invaluable help with the Australia trip; and to my agent, Carolyn Swayze, whose enthusiasm and good humour initiated this book.

The support of the BC Arts Council, Ministry of Small Business, Tourism and Culture; The Canada Council; and the Canadian Department of Foreign Affairs and International Trade is gratefully acknowledged.

For Vicky Husband, with love and admiration

GIRLS AROUND THE HOUSE

ABSENCE MAKES

MY HUSBAND REFUSES TO GO DOWNSTAIRS. "I HAVE A psychiatric condition," he tells me, "a sudden aversion to everything on the lower level."

Since the lower level is where our three teenage children have their bedrooms and also where his mother in her golden but crusty retirement has her suite, I press for details.

"Every time I descend the stairs I break out in a sweat," Gerry says. "My heart races and I feel sick to my stomach."

"Let's look at this," I offer.

"I don't want to look at it," he says. "I want to escape. A cabin in the woods is more and more appealing. With a galvanized tub for bathing and something to cook on. With a small bed. Maybe a battery-operated tape deck to play some music. That's all. I'd never come out."

"Like a stinking old hermit?" I ask. "One of those sad fellows who hate humanity and live in filth?"

"Sounds good to me."

I remember a girlfriend from high school, Linda Simpson. She had three younger sisters. And her father "lived" in the tool shed behind the house. He came in for meals and showers, but otherwise spent his free time in the shed: reading, listening to the radio, sleeping. There was a stone pathway leading from the back stairs of the main house to the shed, and daffodils and tulips grew along the way. He was a tall man, an ordinary-looking father. I don't know what he did for a living, but I often saw him wearing a suit and tie.

The tool shed didn't contain any garden tools, wheelbarrows or the like. Mr. Simpson had cleaned it out; the tools leaned against the back of the shed under a plastic canopy. Inside the shed it was very tidy: a bed, a writing desk, a rug beside the bed, an electric hot plate and kettle, a jar of instant coffee. I regarded Mr. Simpson nervously, as a slightly weird man, off-putting, embarrassing, even shameful.

No one was allowed inside the shed, not even Mrs. Simpson. I had a close look at Mrs. Simpson when I heard this. Searching for clues, I suppose, as to why her husband would act this way. But Mrs. Simpson was a closed book. And I didn't have the nerve to ask her directly why Mr. Simpson lived in the shed. All I knew about Mrs. Simpson was the way she looked: tall, black permed hair, black-rimmed glasses. And that she worked at the Pink Kitten Beauty Salon as a hairdresser.

Linda got pregnant in Grade Ten and had to quit school. She became a mother at fifteen, married an older boy and divorced him two years later. She'd left our sphere for good, by then. Years later I heard she'd opened a vintage clothing store in Vancouver.

A few months ago I was reading the obituaries in the local paper, as I always do, and came across the name Simpson: John (Jack) Edward Simpson. Everyone was listed in the write-up — still a family, it seemed, still together: the loving wife, Pat; the four daughters; the sons-in-law; several grandchildren. The battle with cancer was mentioned along with thanks to the nurses on Ward C. He died at seventy-eight. No mention was made of his life in the shed.

You wonder about anyone's reasons. Why a man will leave his family but move only a stone's throw away. Why not across town, across the country? I often wondered if Mr. and Mrs. Simpson caught glimpses of one another late at night — she through the kitchen window, he through the window of his shed — and if their eyes met and locked. I longed for them to have some sort of understanding.

It never occurred to me then that Mr. Simpson might find family life a burden, that living in the tool shed was his escape. The fact that his escape was a partial one still intrigues me.

My grandfather, I'm told, was the same. Only with him it wasn't a shed he escaped to, it was the outside world. He was a barber with six children. Every so often, he'd put down his scissors and walk out of his shop, leaving his customers in mid-haircut. He'd be gone three or four days, the story goes, off someplace drinking and gambling. Nobody knew where he went; it seems he just wandered from bar to bar, card game to card game. But after a few days my grandmother and her oldest daughter would go looking for him. They'd usually find him asleep on a bench at the train station. That's as far as he got; he never boarded a train. He'd come home, back to his family and his barber shop, and it would be like nothing had happened. Until the next time. No one in my family had an explanation for why he did this; it was just something that occurred, like a sudden storm: without warning my grandfather would remove the shackles of family and work and be gone.

I suppose he got to a point where he couldn't stand it anymore.

Gerry often says the same words: "I can't stand it." Meaning the kids, his mother, the dog and three cats, the mess, the garbage in the kids' rooms, the steady diet of problem solving as our kids take, he believes, too many years to ready themselves for flight. Even though his mother claims he was twenty-seven when he left home. Twenty-seven! "He doesn't like to admit it," Nana tells me, "but it's the truth."

This interesting fact about my husband once prompted an invitation to a dinner party. The hostess couldn't wait to pounce. We'd just sat down to a plate of salad. "You lived at home for twenty-seven years?" she shrieked. Her hilarity was disconcerting. "Tell me all about it," she coaxed. "Did your mother wash and iron your clothes, fix your favourite meals? Let me guess what that was. Meatloaf? Shepherd's Pie?"

"Yes and no," Gerry said dryly, and would say no more. We never bothered with a return invitation.

His own father had it good. He was a travelling sales-man for Parker Pens; for years he was home only on weekends and holidays. My mother-in-law raised four kids pretty much by herself. But she had the weekends to look forward to. Nana still dreamily remembers those years: "Every Saturday night Dad would take me out for dinner. And he always brought me flowers Friday night."

My friend Rita swears that after twenty years of to-getherness, separate vacations are the answer. "Cheaper than marital counselling," she advises, "and at the end of the vacation, there's always the chance that you'll be longing to see one another, and who knows, maybe even lusting for contact. Absence makes … and so forth. Many couples married for a long time come to an agreement," she says ominously.

This is the same friend who, when told of Gerry's desire for a cabin in the woods, exclaimed, "Just what I've always wanted. A little shed at the foot of the gar-den. I'd live there all the time. It would be wonderful. I'd have a flower basket beneath the one window and fill it with trailing lobelia, alyssum, petunias, ivy, geraniums. Visit the main house occasionally — to fix a meal or apply a band-aid. I'd step over toys and garbage and I wouldn't care at all."

Perhaps my husband really wanted a holiday from me but was too polite to say. Perhaps this shed business was an attempt to generalize the situation, to spare me the awful truth … but what could that awful truth be? We'd certainly not had a holiday together, alone, since I was six months pregnant with Gabby, our second child. Three days at Yellowpoint Lodge playing ping-pong with a pregnant woman can't have been much fun for him, it's true. And since then there's been the issue of the sexy lingerie: the crotchless underpants of my youth recycled as dust rags; the elastic from the black-lace bras tying up the roses. "Marion, what ever happened to the see-through bra I bought you in 1977?" he says wistfully, eyeing its sturdy white replacement.

Then again, perhaps it's the writing. Having a writer around the house can't be easy. "You're never here!" Gerry often says, and he doesn't mean I'm hooting it up on a book tour. Exasperated by my repeated domestic failures — forgetting to buy meat and sugar cubes … again; forgetting to pay the cable bill or pick up one of the kids … again. He points at my head. He's practically speechless, grunting and pointing, as if my crimes were beyond imagining: "There it is! There's the culprit! It's your head! It's … emptee! It's in a … a … book!"

Finally he announced he was starting a Spouses of Writers Support Group, claiming he already had two people eager to join.

"What are you going to do?" I asked nastily. "Meet every second Thursday to hold hands and cry about how awful we are to live with?"

"Yes! Yes!"

The "support group" never got beyond a succession of nights in the pub with Rita's husband, Nick. But maybe that was enough. I imagined their conversation.

"Mine reads while fixing meals," Nick might sniff. "She put too much baking powder in the dumplings and they sucked up all the stew. It was revolting. Even the dog ..."

"That's nothing," Gerry would reply gloomily. "Marion's getting even more obscure. She's writing Haiku fiction now — seventeen paragraphs containing seventeen sentences and each sentence containing seventeen syllables. And she's writing seventeen of them! Says it will take her seventeen years! What for? I want to know. What in God's name for?"

Meanwhile, I struggle on, trying to separate the writing self from the domestic self. I often fail at doing this, so I've taken the billboard approach and attached a helium-filled message balloon to my head. It says: *This is what I do, okay? Look after my family. Write books. Read. Talk to family members. Have friends. Travel a little.*

I should also add: Worry a lot ... about money. When you're a writer, there's either just enough or none at all. Between spans of writing, I do odd jobs — bookkeeping, working on elections, the census, the Court of Revision — just to help keep the lean times from becoming desperate.

When Gerry was threatening "support group," I was reading the early diaries of Virginia Woolf. I was struck by how little domestic work she had to do: She had servants to clean and cook; she had no children. She "scribbled" a little in the morning, was served "luncheon," and then, in the afternoon, "took the air" or saw a play or a concert. Imagine that! In the evenings she and Leonard read.

But women who are writers with families … I'm constantly leaving paragraphs to simmer instead of soup or reading *About Your New Toaster* with as much serious attention as I'd give a book of poems.

Commenting on the recent early death of an Australian writer, a friend remarked, "She raised four kids and she wrote four books. What more do they want from us?"

What my husband wants, I'm sure, is a partner who isn't dazed and weary much of the time, who responds with something other than "Huh? Wha … ?" when asked, "What do you want to do this weekend?" Someone who'll take Noel Coward's advice — "Never let anything artistic stand in your way" — and write a bestseller.

So, after twenty-four years together, I decided it was time for an overhaul. I started with the obvious things first, prowling the house room by room, throwing things out.

Before long the front porch was stacked with household debris: a broken vacuum cleaner; boxes full of *National Geographics* and out-of-print literary magazines; cracked water jugs, plates, mugs; a portable record player that never worked, bought at a garage sale; a ton of clothes and stuffed animals; sleeping bags without zippers, bought cheaply, never lasting.

Gerry loaded this garbage onto the bed of his elderly Ford pickup. "We could do this every Saturday for a year and still have stuff to throw out," he said, almost happily.

Then I said to him: "Let's get rid of everything in the house that's ugly." I felt so refreshed when I said this, picturing us living amongst beautiful things. Everything inside our house, and by implication inside ourselves, pared down to a simple essence. A fine bowl, an exquisitely crafted table.

I was wiping up spilled juice from the floor when I said this, and looked up to find my husband staring at me. I guessed what he was thinking. "No, not me," I said. "I don't mean throwing me out. And besides, you're just as ugly."

We laughed. Thankfully.

But we've yet to rid the house of the aesthetically impure. Ugliness is still with us. A thirty-year-old Danish chest of drawers is a good example. Thrown out by my cousin when she remarried: "I always hated it," she told me, "but it was Ken's (the first husband's). Took me five years to pay it off at Standard Furniture. And I resented every payment."

We've had this cast-off for twenty years. The TV sits upon it in our bedroom; videotapes and books are piled on the rest of its surface; the wood has become dull and stained with fingerprints, spilt tea; it's a fierce collector of dust. Why do we still have it? What dreadful karma has been wafting from it all these years? But replacing this chest of drawers has never been a priority, never made the top of any list.

Maybe if we get rid of this chest of drawers, my husband will feel better. Maybe if we start here …

The symbols we make. When the neighbours' marriage broke down and the husband moved out, his wife got a six-month-old dog from the SPCA and called it by her husband's name, Jeffrey, even though the tag on the dog's collar said "Shadow." We'd often hear the kids screaming at the dog: "Jeffrey, you idiot!" It was a Border Collie-cross who liked to sit on top of things, especially the roof of the house, and who frequently wandered off. In the evenings, we'd hear the wife plaintively calling the dog: "Jeff-rey. Here, Jeffrey. Come home, Jeffrey."

That dog was a heartbreak to have in the neighbourhood. It's not surprising that he wandered off, never to return. Being the reviled Jeffrey when he was truly Shadow must have been an overwhelming burden for him.

About relationships, our daughter Lee occasionally gets in the mood to talk. She's coming on seventeen and her curiosity is almost exclusively about male-female relationships. She's reflective during these conversations, not so much revealing what's going on in her own life as wanting information.

A while back she asked: "Who lives longer, men or women?"

Never missing an opportunity to provide her with

statistics from the wider world, I told her that presently women are favoured to live longer than men, but that this advantage has been diminishing because of increases in cigarette smoking and stress levels amongst women.

But she didn't want to hear this. Cutting me off in mid-sentence, she said, "I heard women live longer because men have to work so hard during sex."

"Who told you that?"

"I don't remember. Is it true?"

And I'm picturing cool, languid girls with sweating, grunting boys sliding from their bodies like exhausted lizards.

"Well, is it true?" she demands.

"Could be," I tell her, forcing myself to think generally, to think about *women in general* and not about her and her friends on Friday nights.

So this is the year for an overhaul, I tell my husband. But what else can we throw out besides broken vacuums and ugly furniture? Not the children, surely; they'll fly when they're ready. Not Nana, surely; she locks her door because things were never so ruinous in her day. She worked and worked to ensure that there were clean laundry rooms, clean children. Not me. I mostly let them be, and now and then they rise to our upstairs domain, to our blue-and-white and tea-stained world, to share a meal, an idea, a dream.

"All the glasses and cereal bowls are missing," Gerry has been announcing lately. Disgust and scorn in his voice. He's taken to hiding his favourite mug.

The spoons have disappeared, too, I might have added. Lost in the basement rooms where the children, Leslie, Gabby and Lee, feed on quesadillas and videos in preparation for grown-up life. They're having a kind of moratorium, I've come to believe — though, it's true, some might call it a free lunch.

This is what Gerry hides: his razor, his mug, his money, his tobacco and papers, his chocolate bars, his wine, his lunch-meat (in the freezer behind the bagels).

This is what I hide: my eyeshadow, my eyeliner pencil, my dental floss, my money, my favourite white shirt, my underpants, my black socks, my nail file, my hairbrush, my toenail polish. More than once I've had to go through a day without socks because (a) I can't remember where I hid my supply or (b) my hiding place has been found out.

The kids have taken to hiding chunks of orange cheese when I buy it. "For our nachos," they tell me, "because Dad eats it all."

My husband is still loathe to venture downstairs. "Have you not noticed the smell?" he asks accusingly.

The smell? Rank and cheesy? Or the other smell? The heavy fumes of spray-on perfume from The Body Shop mixed with the musty odour of thickly applied deodorant and unwashed socks.

I ask Gerry, "Have you considered that your aversion to descending to the lower levels of our house may be symbolic? You know, an aversion to digging deeper into yourself?"

"Not interested in symbols. Or theory. Or motiva-
tion. I just want a cabin in the woods."

And so we leave it at that. Those fleeting — or is it
compelling? — dreams of an isolated cabin surfacing
every so often into our lives, like the rank smell from
the basement, that great underbelly of the house seeth-
ing like a sewer beneath our bed, our marriage bed where
we try to make love between curtain calls. We've become stage managers for those whose lives are occur-
ring before and after us — his mother, the children. On
hand is what we are — helpmates, facilitators to those
in transition. I feel exhilarated when I have this thought,
full of meaning, purpose. I believe I've just discovered
something true. I tell this to Gerry. Lately he's taken to
buying shovels and doesn't want to hear what he calls
my "suspicious insights." So far he's bought three large
shovels. They lean against the house unused, their galvanized steel pristine and shiny. "None of the kids will
ever take them!" he tells me triumphantly and has a good
laugh imagining them working up sweat with a shovel.

I wonder if he has in mind a return to gardening. (The
kale in the vegetable patch is still reseeding and feeding
the finches after all these years.)

But, no, he says, the shovels are not for gardening.
And he'll say no more.

A couple of times I've caught him in the early evening
standing before his shovels and smiling blissfully.

And then it occurs to me: He's going to build an
escape tunnel; he's a prisoner of war and he's going to

tunnel his way out of the family home. Or maybe dig the foundation for his "cabin in the woods." One Saturday morning I'll find him hard at work in the backyard. I'll be watching from the kitchen window. He'll glance up from his labours and smile at me and he'll be happy. A little cabin with a hot plate, a single bed and a galvanized tub is what he's probably thinking. And I'm thinking, as I wave at him from behind the kitchen window, how thrilling it will be when the cabin's completed and, after several months of hermitage, he finally invites me in.

SKIDNEY

NANA PLAYS BRIDGE WEDNESDAY NIGHTS AT THE SIDNEY Silver Threads. She's usually home by ten, but this week she came through the door at eight forty-five. Came into our bedroom, flushed and excited, and announced, "They evacuated the centre! Gas leak!"

This was better than any disaster show on TV.

"There were sixteen tables of bridge," she told us, "and suddenly we could smell gas. Howard, the director, called the fire department and then asked the players: 'You can either carry on with the bridge game or you can go home. What do you want to do?' And everyone yelled in one voice, 'Play bridge.'"

When I heard this, I immediately wrote the *National Enquirer* headline: Seniors Elect to Play Bridge in Death Trap.

And why wouldn't they? When you're seventy, or eighty, or ninety, why not play bridge in the midst of a potential explosion? It makes sense: It's a literal chance to go out with a bang. Possibly the last chance. And it's the opposite of those sad people who quit smoking a week before they die of lung cancer or who abandon their daily ration of cinnamon buns and take up weight training at age eighty-eight.

But the bridge players' thrill had been short-lived. A fireman dressed in a yellow and black rubber suit, a yellow helmet, and with an oxygen tank strapped to his back stood at the doorway to the bridge room and bellowed, "Evacuate! Now!"

"It was so exciting," Nana said. "Outside there were fire trucks and police cars with their lights flashing. And the road on either side of the centre was closed off with that yellow tape you see on the news. What they use when there's a murder."

This is about as exciting as Sidney gets.

True, there's the Sidney Days Parade on July 1, followed by the giant sidewalk sale down Beacon Avenue. And there's the Santa Claus Parade, where local businesspeople attach helium-filled balloons to their minivans and holler at the shivering crowd, "Ten percent off blinds at Fashion Focus Paint & Accessories!"

But exciting?

This year the Santa Claus Parade included our son Leslie's band playing live music from the back of a flatbed truck. They had seven blocks in which to impress the crowd. When they passed by us, the band was in the pause between songs. What we got was some amp noise. Seven blocks go by fast, even at the pace of a parade. My husband only got one blurred picture of our son's back while he was tuning his guitar.

The band's other guitarist took thirty minutes off work

at The Pantry, where he's a short-order cook, so he could be in the parade. How small town, I thought. I pictured him throwing off his greasy apron and running out of the restaurant at the last moment. Climbing onto the back of the truck as it began the parade and hastily donning his denim rock-star hat and carefully ripped jacket for his instant identity change.

It's like the volunteer fire department. The man who's filling your tank at the gas station could, moments after the alarm sounds, be the same man hanging off the back of a wailing fire truck.

Sidney really is a small town — a small town on a largish island. The main street, Beacon Avenue, veers off the Pat Bay Highway, a four-lane road whose main purpose is to link Victoria with the ferry terminal to the mainland. Day and night, cars scream past Sidney, trying to make the ferry a couple of miles down the road. You can picture the panicked ferry-goers clawing at their car windows. "A cute island, yes, but let us off RIGHT NOW!"

Take a breath, you want to call out. There'll be ferry lineups, delays, and what's so great about Vancouver? This is much the same message Sidney's town officials have tried to convey. Hoping to share in the tourist money that Victoria attracts, they've spiffed the place up with paving-stone sidewalks and nautical-style street signs. A billboard on the highway before you reach the town announces hopefully, "Welcome to Beautiful Sidney by the Sea."

Those of us who live in or around Sidney agree it's a beautiful place. But many of us are glad the tourists largely ignore the town — we like it quiet and dull — and wish the officials would cease their relentless advertising campaigns. It's embarrassing. It's pathetic. It's like the time when I was ten years old and travelling in Oregon with my family. Driving through a small town, we passed a rundown motel. A woman wearing an apron and a girl about my age rushed out from the motel and stopped our car. They looked desperate. "Please," the woman said, "stay here! We'll give you a really good rate."

My father couldn't drive away fast enough.

Sidney's town officials are trying to make Sidney into a travel destination. But you wonder if there really are excited families in Montana or Manitoba or Japan or New York planning a dream vacation to Sidney. This is just not a place you save up to visit. Maybe, if the weather's good, you stop in for an hour or two on your way from Victoria to the ferry, poke around the nautical theme shops and Tanner's Books and maybe take a stroll along the newly invented Port Sidney to look at the boats. But you won't stay here for long. Where's the theme park? Where's the mall? Where's the world's largest stuffed salmon?

We do have our eccentrics, but what town doesn't?

We have our very own street performer who stands outside the liquor store next to Safeway, an aged hippie who was quoted in the *Sidney Review* as saying, "I just want to love everybody."

He wraps an old, red velvet curtain around his waist, puts an opera tape in his portable boom box and does a puppet show using hand-held puppets. When he's not performing, he can be seen riding around Sidney on his bike, wearing leather shorts and a waist-length, royal-blue satin cape made by the town's other eccentric, a ninety-five-year-old seamstress who lives in the world's tiniest house.

The house, painted light green and trimmed in white, is about the size of an average kitchen. Inside, the walls are covered floor to ceiling with clothes on hangers, some of the clothes seventy years old. They're clothes that the still-working seamstress has made for people but that were never collected.

There's an idea. *Visit Sidney. Home of the world's tiniest functioning house!*

A lot of condos have been built in Sidney during the last few years, and they're mainly occupied by seniors. Once, a few years ago, driving Lee along Beacon Avenue to the dentist, she screamed, "Omigod, look at all the old people!" It was nine-thirty on a Tuesday morning and she'd just had a seniors sighting. Never before had she seen so many at one time; they're rarely on the streets after three p.m., when school's out.

Sidney also has its writers and poets, quite a few of them.

A writer friend told me, "I went into the post office with the manuscript of my novel and the man behind the counter said, 'New novel? What's it about?' The next day the checkout woman at Sidney Super Foods asked me, 'When's the new book out?' Do you think these people actually talk about us?"

Yes.

I've had the same experience. A new server in Lunn's Bakery has an Australian accent. Because I'd just been there, I said, "Are you from Australia?" Right away her co-worker warned her, "Watch what you say. She's a writer. It might end up in a book."

When I made an appearance at the local book club, the hostess said, "We're going to make you sign something before we start. So you won't write about anything that's said here." She was only half-joking.

Another sign idea: *Warning. Sidney ahead. Writers on the loose.*

Our kids' name for Sidney is Skidney. A place light years away from the town inhabited by the handful of writers, the penny-conscious seniors, the young families in their starter homes.

When I hear the word Skidney I naturally think of Skid Row, a despairing place filled with drunks, addicts and the homeless. But what the kids mean by Skidney is that it's a rough, down-home, beer-drinking, unpretentious place. Skidney is a state of mind.

"In Skidney, when you go to a party," a neighbourhood teenager told me, "you hold onto your beer. Actually *hold onto it*. There's all these kids standing around talking or dancing and they'll have cases of beer stuck under their arms. No one's crazy enough to put them down because they'll get taken. So the thing is, you hold onto them no matter what. A lot of girls wear packs and put their beer in there. People at Skidney parties are always coming up to you and trying to bum a beer. You look in your case and say, 'Hey man, I've only got eight left. Sorry.' If you put your beer down even for a minute, it's gone. That's Skidney."

Our daughter Gabby offers her version of Skidney:

"There was this hardcore Barbie chick and she's, like, in the bowling alley with Mike Panowski. And she's supposedly his new girlfriend from Victoria? And I couldn't believe it. She thinks I'm hot on Mike because we're talking and it's weird how every time it's my turn to bowl it's his turn, too. But I mean, like, *Mike*? Duh. But this Barbie chick keeps staring at me. Like a serious, big-time, jealousy trip. She's got these platform shoes on and tight black pants and perfect, wispy little bits of blonde hair pulled out of her ponytail. And she finally says to Mike before they've even finished their game, 'C'mon Mike, like, we're leaving.' And then she comes over to our table, all fake smiles, and puts this half-pitcher of beer in front of me and says, 'Like, here, you can have this.' And we're like, wow, thanks, that's really cool! And it took Charlotte and me half an hour to figure it out. We were supposed to be insulted. Like, in the Barbie chick's world this was an insulting thing to do. And it was such a laugh. Because in our world, in Skidney, this is the coolest thing you can do. Hey, you want to give us some free beer? Right on!"

I grew up in Cordova Bay, some ten miles down the road from Sidney. A place our kids refer to as "preppy."

"Kids in Cordova Bay blow-dry their hair and wear *fashions*," Leslie tells me disgustedly. "And they don't drink beer. At parties everyone puts their wine on the kitchen counter like grown-ups. When kids from Skidney go to one of their parties, the wine's gone in seconds."

When I was a brawling young person, my friends and I often went "slumming" at the Sidney Hotel. We'd drink beer and watch the fights in the "Beer Parlour," a large, noisy, brightly lit, smoky room filled with small round tables covered in red terrycloth. Each table had as many glasses of beer as it could hold — twenty or thirty glasses — and beer was twenty-five cents a glass. Around eleven or twelve in the evening there'd always be a drunken fight or two, and the police would come. My Cordova Bay friends and I imagined we were seeing the wild side of life, and it was thrilling.

"That's nothing," Gabby said when she heard this story. "A couple of fights? Like, how protected!"

In Skidney, I'm told, everyone meets in the Safeway parking lot around seven on a Friday or Saturday night to discover where the party is. Then they leave en masse. Imagine thirty or forty kids arriving on your doorstep, looking for a party. Imagine if they were certain they had the right address.

Last Halloween, Gerry drove seven costumed girls to a party up the road. The girls weren't actually invited, but it was "cool" because they knew someone who knew someone who was having the party. It was an outdoor party, and you had to wear a costume.

Seven girls piled into the back of his pickup: a clown, a spider, a hooker, a Hawaiian in a pink wig, a New Age guru in a blue wig and white gown, a nymph wearing a crown of leaves, and a Raggedy Ann. Their packs bulged with cans of beer.

As they were pulling out of the driveway, one of the girls yelled to my husband, "Do you mind if I light this?"

Gerry, glancing in the rearview mirror, saw what he thought was a monster joint. "Yes!" he croaked, sweat forming on his upper lip. It turned out to be a Roman candle.

"Lighting that would have been even worse," he said when he returned home. He also said, "I can't believe I did that. Driving seven minors in possession of alcohol in the back of my truck. Thank Christ the police were busy searching delinquents for dope at the community bonfire."

"You go to a Skidney party," Leslie tells us, "and by ten o'clock most everyone's drunk and puking, drunk and screaming, or passed out."

"Sounds like the good old days to me," Gerry said.

For a year or two before I met him, Gerry was a regular at the Sidney Hotel. There are guys he drank with then who are still hanging around the local bars on a full-time basis. Guys who never went anywhere. In their forties and fifties now, they're either on welfare or working part-time in construction. If it's summer, they're maybe stripping boats at one of the local marinas. Their backs are gone, their knees are gone, and if they ever had them, so are their families. The thing is, they never got out of Sidney.

Never getting out of Sidney is something our kids fear. What I hope they mean by this is: never getting beyond being what they call "a boozing loser."

We stayed in Sidney, Gerry and me, so in a sense we never got out either. But then, we moved on, I tell the kids, *in other ways*. "It doesn't matter where you live. What matters is how you look at things, how you experience your lives."

They get quiet when I talk like this. They don't want to think ten years down the road. They want to think tomorrow. And maybe the day after that — Friday night! They want to believe right now will last forever.

And what I believe is: What else is there to do with youth but spend it fast?

We live in the Deep Cove area of Sidney. There's a small beach at the foot of our hill where, in summer, Gerry and I swim with our dog Mutz in the late afternoons. When the kids were small, before "Skidney" ever existed for us, they swam there, too. Those were years of riding on logs in the water and building castles on the sandbar, of seaweed fights and water skiing behind a neighbour's boat. And running up the hill late for supper, their beautiful suntanned bodies covered in fine, grey sand. Then flinging their inner tubes, their masks and snorkels, their wet towels, onto the deck. Hosing themselves off before racing inside.

Now there's a new generation of young kids doing the same thing. And everyone down at the beach knows all the connections: whose kid belongs to whom and where, exactly, they live. And isn't it great, everyone says, that Kira's grandmother at eighty-two still swims every day?

The main topic of conversation amongst the swimmers has never changed: water temperature. "How's the water today?" you might ask someone who's just towelling off. What you'll hear is anything from "Beautiful!" to "Freezing. It'll make your bones ache."

Over the years, we've learned to tell the temperature of the water just by looking at it. Clear means cold; cloudy means warm. And the warmest water is when it has a greenish-brown tinge to it, an algae bloom. We're always telling dubious newcomers, "No, that's *not* pollution. It's a red tide. The swimming will be great!"

More than once, Stan, a wiry senior citizen who lives in a waterfront house, has bounded down the beach when he sees us taking off our shoes and arranging our towels on the sand. When he makes such a determined visit, we know what he's going to say. "Hey there, folks," he'll call a good fifty feet before he reaches us. "Did you hear that teenage party down here last night?"

"No!" we'll say, acting shocked by the very idea. We know he suspects our kids. But we want him to think they spend every waking moment volunteering at the hospital or attending Bible camp or walking the dogs of invalids.

Once, he'd asked about another party. "It was coming from up your way," he said, jerking his head in the direction of our house. "The music was so loud. All we could hear was this thumping sound. Thump. Thump. Thump."

"Must have been my mother," Gerry said brazenly. "She had a few of the ladies in for bridge last night. Must have put on Frank Sinatra. She's eighty-one, but you know how these old girls like to have fun!"

"Hah! Eighty-one you say? Golly!"

It was, of course, our party — fourteen of our friends ripping up the carpet to the House sounds of Matthew Herbert Herbert and Bob Sinclair.

About the teenage beach party, Stan pressed on. "You didn't hear it?" he asked, incredulous. "That surprises me. The music was so *loud*. And there was yelling and girls in the water screaming. You didn't hear it up at your place?"

"We must have slept through it," Gerry said, bored and picking up a stick for the dog. The dog, excited, turning in circles across the sand to the water.

"Gosh, it was loud," Stan continued. "I would have thought you'd hear it at your house. No? I was down here this morning picking up empty beer bottles. Some of them broken. The garbage they left! I picked up half a dozen empty chip bags and cigarette packs."

"Wasn't that good of you?" I said, and my husband shot me a glance.

"Yes, well. At ten-thirty I called the RCMP. Can you believe this? They couldn't come because of a house party in Sidney. Got out of control."

After Stan left to fling himself in the water and float on his back, Gerry, pretending not to talk to me, stared at the water and whispered out the side of his mouth, "Where were they last night?"

"At a house party in Sidney," I replied, gazing placidly at the tiny windsurfers in the distance. Then added, "But not at the rowdy one. Another one."

Gerry sighed. "So it wasn't them down here."

"No."

"Well, that's something."

"They've said they won't party at our beach."

"And you believe that?"

"Yes. This beach is a special place for them. They love this beach. They won't do anything to wreck it."

"I'm getting tired of Stan," my husband said.

That day we went for our usual swim. Gently parting the seaweed as we breaststroked along the shore, the dog beside us, the water was "Fantastic!" "Beautiful!" "Like soup!" A few swimmers on the beach were stretched out on their towels, drying off in the sun. Toddlers and their older brothers and sisters played with plastic boats at the water's edge.

While over in Skidney, our kids were having a respite from paradise, tearing up the town with their awful young lives.

CONDOM RUN

I STOPPED IN AT THE BIRTH CONTROL CLINIC. I WAS MAKING a "condom run," as Gerry calls it. The waiting room was filled with sweaty, sullen girls reading *People* and *Vogue* and chewing on the orange and black jujubes that are left in a plastic bowl on the reception counter.

Staff at the Birth Control Clinic have tried to make it a cheerful place. In the waiting area there are two colonial-style chesterfields draped with knitted afghans. Several stuffed animals sit on a wooden rocking chair. And the walls are painted a sunny yellow and decorated with bright posters about the symptoms of sexually transmitted diseases, the importance of using condoms. One poster has a provocative title: 100 Ways To Make Love Without Having Sex. I had a closer look — it took some determined reading because the print was so small — but the list included going for beach walks at midnight and having long talks about "life."

The women who work in the Birth Control Clinic are all middle-aged or older, and every one of them is exuberantly friendly — an odd personality contrast to their clients, who are close-mouthed, even hostile.

The girls in the waiting room usually give me a sour look when I drop in, but I'm not deterred by their scorn because I'm on a mission. I'm hoping that the three young people who call our basement "home" will eventually consider personal responsibility as a life option. In the meantime, there's someone looking out for them.

Consumed with purpose, I fill my bag from the bowls of foil-covered condoms that are placed here and there about the room like appetizers at a party.

"Take as many as you like!" the woman behind the desk gaily tells me. And I realize that this woman and I are of one mind — zealots and pragmatists alike when it comes to the health and safety of our children.

I stuff perhaps fifty condoms into my purse, calculating with difficulty how many condoms per young person per week will be needed. This is difficult, because when it comes to the sex lives of our children, I can only guess what's going on. It's one of those taxing concepts like trying to imagine the end of the universe. The mind stretches and it hurts.

It's my custom to do a condom run every month or so. I add it to my list of things to do on a particular Friday afternoon. I'm rigid in my shopping habits: Friday is the only day I'll take myself away from things literary to do the grocery shopping. If we run out of frozen juice or cream cheese and bagels before then, I'm deaf to criticism. The cries of *"There's nothing to eat!"* that I routinely hear by Wednesday and Thursday have no effect on me.

I tell everyone, virtuously, "If all the juice is gone, drink water." And so on.

It shouldn't be surprising, then, that there's a crowd on hand Friday afternoons waiting for my return from the grocery store. And not only our kids ... their friends, too. Word has gotten out. The feeling in the air is celebratory, like it is on Christmas or birthdays. And all because there are eight to ten bags of groceries in the trunk of my car.

"Did you get any orange cheese?" our twenty-year-old son Leslie asks while unloading the car. There's a high degree of anxiety in his voice. He pays room and board now, so feels entitled to question my purchases. Only last week he left an angry note for me on the kitchen counter: "DO NOT JUST BUY ONLY LEMONADE!!!"

This is the son who announced, when he turned nineteen, that he was moving out to live with his rock band. My husband immediately went and bought a bottle of expensive French wine to celebrate. "Never in my wildest dreams did I think he'd move out so *soon*." He sounded positively giddy uncorking the wine. "I thought we'd have him *forever*!"

As moving day approached, Gerry and I visited the paint store, spending an exhilarating ten seconds choosing the first cream colour we saw on the paint palette. Our plan was to repaint Leslie's bedroom.

"You know," Gerry said, driving home from the paint store, "we haven't seen his walls for years! All those upside-down posters. Why did he put them like that, anyway? And think of the garbage we'll get to throw out!"

He spent the rest of the day happily looking around the house and the yard for the paint tray.

As moving day neared, Nana bought Leslie a set of dishes for his "new place." We made a special trip to Zellers and spent the morning consulting with one another over dish styles. "It's important to have good things," Nana declared, finally choosing an earthenware "starter" set, white with blue trim.

The new place was a rundown shack in Sidney. It was going to be the home of three of the four members of Leslie's band. The band's name, I CAN'T STAND YOU, was scrawled on the outside front wall in large black letters. Inside the house: a vast collection of beer cans; two broken chesterfields; a gray arborite kitchen table and two chairs; a bathroom with a broken shower; two tiny bedrooms and three single mattresses; a set of drums and three very large amps.

"We can save money by using the place for jamming," Leslie told us, indicating that he at least understood the principles of personal budgeting. "Now we won't have to rent a separate jamming spot."

He was, it appeared, unconcerned about the fact that the police station was a block down the road.

"Won't be a problem," he explained, when I pointed out things like noise and late-night parties. "All the neighbours are really old and take sleeping pills. They won't hear a thing." He named the new place "The Shack."

The day before the move, I took Leslie grocery shopping.

"To start him off," I told Gerry. He looked at me dubiously.

That night we had a send-off dinner where Nana tearfully remembered every family member who had ever left home. "I just cried and cried watching them go out that door," she said, repeatedly. "To think of them so young and alone in the world ..."

"He's only ten minutes away, for god's sake!" Gerry said.

"Yeah," Leslie said, shoving the celebration barbecue steak into his mouth. "I'll come and visit now and then. You can make me tea."

Gabby asked, "Can I use his room as a den? You know, put in a chesterfield and TV and have parties in there?"

We told her no, it would be a guest room. Just saying "guest room" made me feel exalted; we'd never had such a thing before.

I cried on moving day. "So young and alone," I kept thinking.

At noon Gerry called from work. "Has he gone yet?"

"He's still in bed."

"For Christ's sake!"

I went downstairs to Leslie's bedroom. He was asleep in a nest of quilts and pillows. His cat, Bob, was lying on his back, purring. The walls were bare, the shelves gutted. A cardboard box beside the bed was filled with clothes.

"Shouldn't you be up and leaving?"

Leslie came awake, mumbling from beneath a pillow, "Yeah, later."

I gazed fondly at our firstborn. A young man with

focus, with a determined set of "life goals." After a year of university, he'd decided to work in a restaurant and devote his life to the band. When this decision was announced, Gerry, who was certain our son would become a professional soccer player, or at the very least a high school PE teacher, said to me, "Congratulations, Marion! We've just given the world another dishwasher."

But Leslie eventually moved out. It took the rest of the day. The actual moving-out part — loading his belongings into his car — took maybe ten minutes. The rest of the time was spent drinking tea, using our CD player "one last time," playing with his cat (who wasn't accompanying him), washing his sizable collection of polyester slacks from Value Village, the ones he buys in the extra-large size then flamboyantly cinches to his six-foot, 142-pound body. (They hover on his hips a good four inches below his flannel boxer shorts, and I always have to control myself when he wears those pants because I want to sneak up and, shrieking hysterically, pull them down.)

As for cleaning out his room, I was relieved to see he'd taken the two hundred packs of condoms I'd left on his bedside table. I'd made a special "run" for them.

"Two hundred condoms? A bit excessive, don't you think?" Gerry said.

"Well ..." I sniffed. "Well ..."

The next day my husband painted the empty bedroom. "Leave me alone," he told me when I offered to help. "I want to do it myself. I'm anticipating a peak experience."

The first weekend after our son's move we had a house guest, a young poet from Vancouver who was in town to give a reading. The new guest room looked beautiful: cream walls, vacuumed rug, a window you could actually see through, a single bed covered with a white Hudson's Bay blanket. Even the poet appreciated the room; when we took her down there she said, "A good place to do some reading" and flung her pack on the bed.

"What are you reading?" I asked.

"Derrida," the poet said, a challenging tone in her voice.

The next morning we found her asleep on the upstairs chesterfield. This was startling because the chesterfield is right outside our bedroom. It's the place our kids always go when they're sick — a holdover from their younger days, a gesture of being closer to us in time of need. I thought maybe the poet had had a nightmare. Or was frightened sleeping alone in the downstairs room. Being from the city, maybe she was spooked by so much silence. Or maybe she was sick.

Controlling my need to feel her forehead, I let her sleep. We tiptoed around her for much of the morning. She looked sweet lying there, her face pink and sweaty. Like one of our kids, really. She'd carted a pillow and the Hudson's Bay blanket upstairs with her. Her socked feet hung over the end of the chesterfield. She looked very comfortable. And Derrida was nowhere in sight.

The dog's barking woke her at eleven-thirty.

"Are you all right?" I asked.

Yes, she was fine, she told us crankily, now that she'd had some sleep. It was the girls in their room next door keeping her awake. Sneaking in their window at midnight, they'd carried on laughing and watching TV until four in the morning.

We apologized, gave the poet breakfast and took her to the ferry.

When we got back, Leslie's battered red Maverick was in the driveway. We found him in bed in the guest room.

"I've got a sore throat," he groaned. "And there's nothing to eat at The Shack. Can you make me some tea?"

I had a talk with Gabby and Lee. "That was very inconsiderate of you, keeping our guest awake like that. And how many times have I told you there's no need to climb in the bedroom window? You can walk through the mud-room door like normal, grown-up people. Only fourteen-year-old babies climb through windows. You're both well past that now. This is what you do: You take off your shoes and tiptoe quietly down the stairs to your room. It's an ages-old tradition."

Ten days later Leslie moved back home. "Do you even *know* how expensive it is out there?" he asked accusingly, citing as evidence an "unreal" phone bill and the fact that "all of Sidney" was eating out of their fridge. He'd been gone for eighteen days in total.

"Eighteen days of bliss," Gerry sighed, watching him unload his car.

"He obviously wasn't ready," I said.

"Uncle Jimmy moved in and out at least a dozen times before he left home for good," Nana said happily. She was standing with us on the front porch.

Our son grinned at the three of us as he struggled past with his TV set. He didn't seem at all embarrassed about returning home so soon.

After everything was back in his room, Nana invited all of us into her downstairs suite for tea. While Leslie munched contentedly on the cookies his grandmother had made and stored in advance for this occasion, my husband whispered to me: "One move down, eleven to go."

Later, after poking his head into Leslie's room, he announced, "The posters are back on the walls. Right way up this time. I guess that's something."

I went and had a look. Everything was as before, only cleaner. The box of dishes, unopened, was shoved in the closet. The TV was back on the dresser, the cat was asleep on the bed. Only the condoms weren't in evidence. I'd had in mind sneakily counting how many of the two hundred were left. In this way, my condom calculations might be more accurate.

"Um," I said, interrupting our son watching *Soccer Saturday*. "Um ... where are all the condoms I left?"

"The girls took them," he said. "They've been selling them at school. Didn't you know? They were choked about not having condom machines in the washrooms. It's some protest thing they're having about student rights. They've made signs. You'll probably be getting a call about it next week from the school ..."

THE PRINCESS, THE QUEEN & THE WITHERED KING

A Tale from Wit's End

THERE'S A PLACE CALLED "WIT'S END," AND I LIVE THERE.
It's a black place filled with guilt and accusation, practically a storybook place. A place where evil queen mothers dwell, disguised as humpbacked, hand-wringing crones. Supremely ugly, eternally disgusting. Every princess knows to avoid them, has been trained from birth to revile them, these victims of makeovers in reverse, these controlling, fun-sapping mothers. Nightly we crawl into our miserable holes, lick our festering wounds and prepare for next day's battle.

The battlefield awaits. It's the breakfast table and the queen is screaming: "You've got two minutes before your ride leaves for school!!" Spit flying, eyes bulging.

The princess is serene, applying mascara before a compact mirror, her cereal uneaten. "Calm down," she growls.

Already the king is in the car, honking the horn. There's a king? Yes, my god, poor thing — a hairless, skinny king, reduced to muteness, reduced to tossing his eyes at the ceiling. His eyes, these days, regularly exploding out of his head like champagne corks. The ceiling bruised, a moonscape. He's in the car now, backing it up, grimly asserting what's left of his kingness.

The queen hears the threatening crunch of tire on gravel. Oh no! Her lips purse into a million wrinkles (so ugly!), her heart is racing (such uselessness), her hands are damp (wet claws). "Alright," she snaps, "miss your ride, be late for school ... fail English ..." Snapping like a half-mad terrier. Snap, snap.

The princess, still unconcerned, saunters out the door barefoot, boots in hand, stopping before the kitchen window to have a last look at her lovely self, then wanders up the drive to the retreating car. The pathetic queen on the front porch calling, "Say goodbye!" The princess deigning to speak without turning her head: "Yeah, whatever."

The face of a mother in battle is not pretty: red eyes, blotchy skin, the lines around the mouth etched in grimness. The daughter, on the other hand, is radiant — haughty, aloof, flushed with health, adept at tossing her head in pity and disdain.

Here at Wit's End, her father and I huddle, snatch anxious consultations in the bathroom, whisper over the supper table. Eye contact, imperceptible nods becoming an art form of understated communication. The battles are fast paced, the manouevring tricky. Unpredictable mortar attacks from unpredictable demands can occur at any moment. ("Can I have that peach cooler in the fridge for breakfast?"; "I'm moving to Arizona to be a waitress — so what if I'm fourteen?") Everything is liable to happen. To not happen. Morning storms are the worst, when her mood is not even civil, when demands are the strongest, responses nasty. Nasty. A word that's suddenly on our lips, hauled from the depths. A word in waiting. Amazing how it fits everything. "That was a nasty look." "I don't like the nasty tone of your voice." "Why must you be so *nasty*?" From the Dutch word *nestig*, meaning dirty. Yes, the fighting is dirty, sly.

The queen's nose is twitching. The princess has just returned to the castle and floated through the living room, where the queen is lying on the couch reading How To Deal With Your Acting-Up Teenager. *There's a certain smell ...*

Today the princess's hair is a shade of orange; she's wearing the king's Christmas boxer shorts — red Santas on a green background — hiking boots and a yellow nylon jacket, never seen before, the kind, the queen believes, maniacs wear.

The queen's nose is twitching, but she's about to use a new strategy, throw the princess off guard: She's going to use the word "darling." As well, following the book's advice, she's going to appear as languid and lovely as her daughter. (But there's that smell ...)

"Hello, darling," the queen says, her breath studied, dreamy. "Where did you get the jacket?"

"Wha...?" the princess says, momentarily arrested. "Who...?"

Once upon a time, long long ago, the queen got ripped. Many, many times. So many times, in fact, that this present, certain smell hovering about her daughter takes her back. But not to fourteen. At fourteen the queen remembers going to movies, having pyjama parties, curling her girlfriend's hair, giggling about boys ... Her mind wasn't twisted, blown or dulled until she was well on in age —

twenty, twenty-one.

The queen is being cunning, hoping she sounds bored. "Darling," she asks, "what's that smell on you?"

A brief look of panic disturbs the princess's lovely countenance, her glassy eyes focus, stare down at the strangely relaxed queen.

The princess says, "I hate it when you're like this. You're so ... .so ... different ..."

The queen smiles at her daughter's retreating back. Satisfaction. Score one for the queen. Now if only she could maintain this course ... What does the book say?

The book says: "Give them responsibility for their own lives." "Stand up for yourself." "Assert your rights." "Steal centre stage." "Don't be sucked into giving them negative attention..."

Alright, alright! But at times our daughter's brain power is staggering, and we have to be always on the alert, scanning the skies for incoming missiles. There's the ability she has to set us up, push the right (wrong!) buttons. There's her subtle manipulations, the way she can lie so sweetly, sound so reasonable. "Aha! A foil!" we cry. We know that one: We've done it ourselves; we know how easy it is to lie. Heartless, we were, just like she is, and conniving. Wouldn't I always try to get my way? Do anything, say anything, to go to the party, date the wrong boy?

And the king! The withered king who these days can't even get the dog to obey. At sixteen he had a spare set of keys made for his mother's car. The sneaky future king stealing his mother's car, roaring around town in the small hours, drunk and belligerent.

Three a.m. in the castle. Sleepless again, the queen is at her desk composing a MANIFESTO, *thinking, "Perhaps the light approach . . ."*

Next day the princess reads the MANIFESTO *stuck to the fridge door:*

1. We are firm but reasonable parents; we don't scream (hardly ever) or hit; we simply lay down the rules. Consequences occur if rules are broken.

2. We are open to negotiation. We are not deaf; we are as flexible as grass in the wind.

3. Generally we are loving and kind. Specifically, we encounter periodic emotional disturbances with skill, patience and every street-fighting tactic we can remember.

4. Moment-to-moment resolutions mean nothing, although we cannot ignore the moments. Nevertheless, we will not anticipate bad moments; bad moments will not exist until they are upon us. We will live our happy fulfilled lives, thinking greater thoughts, having calm, enriching emotions, having a multitude of good moments. Breathing deeply. Counting to ten.

5. We will consume alcohol as required: A glass or two of sherry during skirmishes has proven helpful. A bottle of wine per weekend night is de rigeur.

6. Presents and money will be showered upon said young person in adherence to ancient Pavlovian principles: You slobber on cue, you get the treat.

7. We will make every effort to curb our pathological need to utter the words, "NO GODDAMMIT!"

The princess tosses her shining blue hair. "Get a life," she says (would that be scorn in her voice?). "You guys are so pathetic. You think you know what's going on, but you don't."

What's going on? Booze? Drugs? Truancy? Partying at all costs? Hanging out? Scraping through school? Unprotected sex? Or none of this? Just going to movies? Having pyjama parties? Curling her girlfriend's hair? Giggling about boys?

The queen is longing for a bucket of sand in which to stick her head.

When it is said disparagingly of other queens and kings, "Oh, they don't know what's going on ...," the queen thinks: "How wonderful! Not to know what's going on — I'd give anything for a few years of ignorance. I'd give my queendom. I'd give away my keys to the castle if only there were a suitable prince."

Would she? NEVER. There isn't a suitable prince; so far they're all deadbeat, teenage alcoholics whose descriptive vocabularies don't extend beyond the word "fuckin'."

Nevertheless, the princess is howling, her hair, this time, an arresting shade of Kool Aid green, "What's the matter with Hayden? Just because he got kicked out of school, just because he's up on drug charges ..."

People have stopped me on the street, pulled me aside at the grocery store, to tell me how beautiful our daughter is. "She should be a model," they say. "She's gorgeous, a knock-out!" This from the ignorant mothers of sons.

Or from the mothers of grown daughters. These mothers are grinning zombies now, irreversibly brain damaged; they've completely forgotten the battles, the bloodshed at the front door. Then there's the saddest group of all, the new mothers of baby girls, the ones with fear in their eyes. They look at your teenage daughter as if she were an apparition, the stuff of science fiction — a phenonemon, like leprosy, something that could never happen to them.

The queen suspects she might be having a nightmare. She's standing hands out, palms up, before a smug assembly of monarchs. These queens, she knows, consider themselves successful; their princesses do volunteer work, make the honour roll, do math without a calculator, read novels on a Friday night, iron their jeans.

The queen is trying to explain: "But my princess has an incredible mind, she's so fast and articulate. And funny! When she's in the mood she can really make us laugh; she's such a mimic. And don't forget her fashion sense; it's so ... so ... different. And she does love her family, I'm certain of it — the way she always comes home. Given enough time, she'll be wonderful. Right now she's wonderful-in-training ..."

As the queen speaks her words flutter to the ground like pieces of paper, like snapshots. There's that picture of the princess taken during her black period — lips, hair, nails ... another of her at twelve "pretending" to smoke ...

But the assembly of monarchs is angry; they're pelting the queen with family photo albums. "It won't do!" several of them are shouting.

The queen runs for cover. It's either that or being pelted to death with fond memories.

Growing up, how many times did I hear: "You think of no-one but yourself"? I said it myself only yesterday, like some condemned parrot, all teeth and spit. "You don't care if I'm injured (bruised rib from stuck door on family junker), all you want from me is to cut your hair."

Here at Wit's End I'm holding my side in pain. *Pain!* The martyred mother howling neglect, howling the eternal subtext: "You don't love me. If you loved me, you wouldn't … (pick anything)." She's right — it's so pathetic, reviling, this grasping for love. A set-up for rejection.

But what I want to tell her is this: "Remember when I was the best mother in the world? And you were so direct with your love, leaving me notes on my pillow, telling me 'I want to be just like you'? You held yourself up like a mirror, copied everything I did — the way I wore my hair, the way I walked. Oh, I was your idol! And now I've fallen. And it's me who can't abide your departure. It's me, the wicked queen, who would put you to sleep, preserve your childhood sweetness forever."

The king and queen have bought a new secondhand (1982) car. It's a sporty job with a sun roof, finely upholstered seats, doors that easily open and a tape deck that really works. It's a warm spring evening and they're thinking about taking a spin.

The princess, late for dinner again, has just returned home. She's trudging down the driveway, shoulders bent from carrying a backpack that must weigh sixty pounds, filled as it is with every item of clothing that she owns. She's wearing a grey sweatshirt, her head covered with the hood, but it looks as if her hair sticking out the top is purple in colour — the same colour, the queen notes, as the trailing petunias in the garden.

The king and queen are about to get in the car. Lately they're rediscovered one another, have been observed on a Friday evening dancing together in the kitchen. On several occasions now they've left notes on the dining room table that say: "Gone out for dinner. Love XO."

"Your hair ... that's a pretty shade of purple," the queen says to the princess. "Where did you colour it?"

The princess growls, "In the park." Then, narrowing her eyes: "Where are you going?"

"Out for a spin," the king says. "Want to come?"

" ... No." (Was there a hesitation?)

"There's leftover spaghetti in the fridge if you're hungry," the queen adds, smiling.

The king, who's looking like a UN peacekeeper in his blue beret, puts a John Lee Hooker tape in the tape deck and cranks up the volume. The queen backs up the car. In the rearview mirror she can see the princess standing on the front porch, staring. Overwhelmed with love for this rough-edged, beautiful girl, she sticks her hand out the sun roof and waves.

"Where to?" the queen hollers above "Mad Man Blues," and the king hollers back, grinning, "Anywhere. It doesn't matter. Who the hell cares?"

ACTING OUT

THE TERM "ACTING OUT" COMES FROM THE DAYS WHEN GERRY and I worked with emotionally disturbed kids in a residential treatment centre. Whenever a kid ran away, threw a chair through a window, stole money, the young counsellors referred to it as "acting out behaviour," meaning that there was some pain or turmoil in the kid's life that he or she couldn't deal with directly. We counsellors spent a lot of time in meetings trying to determine the source of the acting-out behaviour, certain that "deeper meanings" existed and completely bypassing the notion that I've since come to understand — namely, that stealing a car might have been a lot of fun.

Gerry and I still use the term "acting out." But only indirectly about our kids. Mainly we use it about ourselves. And the meaning is plain, covering all the "deviant," "socially irresponsible" things we do because we can't stand living with them another second. True, our acting out is mild by some standards. Sometimes as mild as drinking wine in front of them at dinner. Or buying asiago cheese and threatening them with expulsion if they so much as smell it.

Or going out for dinner on a recent Tuesday night when we had one acting-out thought in mind: flight.

Me: We're not feeding you tonight.

Them: What do you mean?

Me: We're going out for dinner.

Them: Not seriously? WITHOUT US?

Him: Believe it.

Them: BUT THERE'S NOTHING TO EAT!

Me: There's broccoli. There's tofu. There's butter.

This Tuesday-night dinner out was occasioned not only by the usual list of crimes — mess left in the kitchen; washing machine overloaded so that it bounced itself across the laundry-room floor; wet towels left beside the downstairs shower stall, thereby hastening the time when the soggy floor would collapse from rot — but by three additional torments.

1. Gabby's morning ride to school.

She: (Pulling her sandwich out of the bag.) This is disgusting! How could you make me a ham sandwich?!

Me: (primly) If you don't like the sandwiches I make, you can make your own.

She: I FUCKING WILL.

Me: Good. That's one less thing I have to do.

She: I don't know how you can even make such disgusting lunches. FUCK. AND I'M HUNGRY. I HAVEN'T EVEN HAD BREAKFAST.

Me: Well, if you'd gotten up in time ...

She: I DON'T WANT TO TALK ABOUT IT.

Me: I don't know why you're being so horrible. If you want breakfast, get up when you're supposed to.

My making your lunch for you is a gift ...

She: I TOLD YOU. DON'T TALK TO ME. I'M IN A BAD MOOD.

Me: Well, you can forget about having these special rides to school, too. Get up and go with Dad like you're supposed to.

She: FUCK. I TOLD YOU TO BE QUIET. DON'T TALK TO ME.

2. The arrival of the man from Photo Radar looking for Leslie. This occasioned what Gerry called the best moment of his day because he got to declare with bug-eyed relish: "He's twenty years old! He's an adult! It's his responsibility! It's not my problem!"

"Yes," the man from Photo Radar replied wearily, "we get a lot of that."

3. The appearance of an exuberant, untrained Lab-cross puppy who was being "babysat" by Lee for the evening. "And that will be the last time that happens!" Gerry boomed as we were leaving.

"Do you think they heard you?"

"Just get in the car."

I got in the car. We drove away from the house in silence. You'd think we'd be feeling giddy, escaping as we were, but we were stunned and sullen. Gerry finally said, "I never thought it would come to this. When I was twenty-five years old, I never imagined this future."

"What did you imagine?"

"Independence. Wealth. The Open Road."

There was more silence while I rewrote *Easy Rider*, adding a hip female part for myself and eliminating the final death scene. But keeping the music and the "acid" romp in the graveyard. I tripped out.

Then I said, "My ability to say 'fuck' in a believable fashion came later."

"What are you talking about?"

"The future I imagined for myself. It didn't include a teenage daughter who could scream 'fuck' with such authority. I wanted to stop the car this morning and push her onto the gravel. I would have truly enjoyed that."

"That's what your future didn't include — adolescent girls. But what did you imagine for yourself? When you were twenty-five."

"It was all very vague. Parties. Travelling. Writing. Eventually settling down."

"Well, this is it."

"What?"

"Settling down. This is what 'settling down' looks like. Lifelong harassment by three Frankensteins."

"Not really?"

"Yes, really."

We continued on our way and I thought: Sometimes our life with the kids and my mother-in-law seems like a prison, sometimes it's a joy.

I started feeling guilty about leaving the kids the way we had. "Maybe we should just pick up pizza and take it home with us."

"For Christ's sake, Marion. I thought we were going to Dock 503."

"Sorry. Bad idea. Yes. We'll go to the restaurant. We'll order a bottle of wine. That might help."

"Maybe we should skip dinner altogether," Gerry snarled, "and just go to the liquor store, buy a bottle of wine and sit in front of the post office and drink it."

"We'd be arrested."

"I haven't been arrested since I was thirteen and shot out the street lights with my BB gun." Sudden wistfulness in his voice.

"So your mother's told me at least a hundred times. And you weren't arrested. You were 'talked to' by a very nice law enforcement officer who said you'd go to jail if you did it again. Those are your mother's words."

"I was arrested."

"Okay. You were arrested."

"You're being condescending."

"You're being hostile."

"Buzz off."

"Likewise."

It was raining heavily. We drove past snug-looking houses, containing one happy family after another. I was certain of this. But they're all alike, I reminded myself via Tolstoy. All alike. Because whenever you fall into one of these pits of irritation, everyone else's family life seems better, warmer. Phrases like "They were a close-knit family" loom up to accuse you.

I remembered what a friend had said about living with

young-adult children, kids between the ages of seventeen and twenty-five: "I would never choose them for my roommates. I mean, you're stuck with them. And they're messy and noisy and have all these problems. Like getting jobs. And if they get a job, six weeks is about as long as it lasts. Then it's Unemployment Insurance and they need help getting that because they have to collect all the Employment Records from all the bits of jobs they've had so they can make the twenty qualifying weeks. Then they can't fill out the forms without help or get the cards in on time. Having boyfriends or girlfriends is another issue; they're always falling in love or breaking up. At least once a month it's Heartbreak City. And all their friends are involved and your house is like ER central; CPR is performed on the broken heart by a gang of semi-hysterical friends bearing bottles of rum and the latest rap CD. Next there's the cars. If theirs, they're always breaking down and you know what *that* means. If yours, they're always trying to borrow them.

"And they never have any money; they're always hitting you up for ten or twenty bucks and calling it a 'loan' which they're hoping you'll forget about because you're so old and slow and out of it most of the time. Which is technically true, the result of living with them! Bringing home their down-and-out friends is my personal favourite, because the resident young person gets to practise feeding and caring behaviour at my expense, and when I complain what I get is: 'But you always taught us to have compassion for our fellow human beings!' In fact, 'always' is the operative word here. But I can't go on. It's too depressing."

The restaurant, Dock 503, was a former marina coffee shop remade into an elegant little place with pink table-cloths, fresh flowers on the tables, minimalist lighting. Background music this evening was something classical and mild.

There were fourteen tables in all and only one other couple in the restaurant. But it was early yet, six-thirty. We were shown to a corner table by the window, where a young waiter, impeccably dressed and overly solici-tous, lit the candle. I judged him to be the same age as our son.

"Why is it," I asked my husband, who was blissfully gazing at the cloth-covered menu, "that lately, every time I see a young person doing well, actually working full time, being pleasant to adults and generally seeming to be getting on ... why is it that I feel warm all over? I positively feel love for them."

"Three guesses," he said, catching the waiter's eye.

He was feeling better. He was in the process of trans-forming himself from the harried, threadbare Dad in the beige jacket and jeans into the sophisticated "man of the world," snapper of fingers, orderer of wine, wearer of twelve-hundred-dollar suits.

"I'll have the pepper steak," he declared to the boy waiter. "Rare."

"That way it'll be medium," he later whispered to me, a person who doesn't eat meat. "Order rare and you'll always get medium."

Still, this conversation was a step up from last night's version.

Me: We got cauliflower in the vegetable box this week.

Him: (yawning) Oh? Great.

I ordered the fish, feeling cold and badly dressed, probably tired looking, pale. I couldn't summon up a little black dress and rhinestone earrings for my transformation, or much gaiety either.

Rain pelted against the windows. The young waiters in their black pants and white shirts darted about soundlessly. The place filled up. Now nine of the fourteen tables were taken, each table seating a middle-aged couple. Because it was a Tuesday, I wondered what their home lives might be like. In other words, who were *they* fleeing?

Waiting for our meals, Gerry and I fell into silence. I looked about the room. Some of the couples were talking to one another, but many were not. In the past I'd felt sorry for people like this in restaurants, sitting across from one another in bored silence; I'd assumed wrong things about them, made judgments about their relationships — and my judgments had never been good. Now my husband and I were like them, and, suddenly, I understood: It was a wonderful way to be. Someone in the restaurant was probably looking at us while our food was being served and deciding we were a sad and miserable pair. But we weren't. We were deeply content. We'd gone beyond misery, into the calm and restful state of "neutral." Eating mindlessly. Beside people who were not related to us, who would demand nothing. Eating without telephones ringing or dinnertime squabbles. Temporarily sidestepping the fray. A couple blissfully on hold.

"How's the steak?"

"Okay."

"How's the salmon?"

"Fine."

When we reached dessert, my husband poured the last of the wine and actually stretched as if he'd just awoken from a satisfying nap. He said, "I don't think the adult male is programmed to be involved in child rearing beyond fifteen to twenty years."

"What do you mean?"

"We're not engineered for it biologically. This business of extending childhood into the twenties is a recent phenomenon; it's only been happening since the sixties. Before that, kids were technically adults by fourteen or fifteen, and out working, looking after themselves. Maybe it's different with women. But for men, we run out of interest and energy after fifteen to twenty years. As far as raising the kids is concerned."

"What are you saying?"

"I'm saying I have maybe eighteen months of child rearing capability left in me."

"That's not much time."

"That's too much time."

"And then what?"

"Then I won't care."

"You mean our acting-out days will be over?"

"Yes. As far as the kids are concerned."

"You mean we'd go out for supper just because we wanted to? Not because we were driven?"

"Yes."

"You mean we'd plan ahead? It wouldn't be a knee-jerk decision?"

"Yes."

"I like it. Why don't we do that now? Sort of practise for the end."

"The end?"

"The end of active child rearing. Not the *big* end," I hastened to add, remembering Gerry's fear of Old Age Pensioners. "Fear," he says, because it reminds him that he's on the cusp. "We could take control now," I continued. "Instead of acting beleaguered ..."

"It's no act."

"Okay. Instead of reacting all the time."

"Taking control. I'll go along with that. I'll just say 'no' to everything."

"We don't have to put up with anything we don't choose to," I added, remembering the advice of every how-to book on child rearing I'd read over the years.

"Choice theory," Gerry declared. To his credit: several tonnes of psychology texts.

"Yes. Or 'proactive behaviour.' You know, planning ahead. Taking back your life."

"You sound like you're selling mutual funds."

"Well?"

"We've got nothing to lose."

"So how about lunch next week? You know, just you and me and a veggie lasagne."

"I'd rather fly to Paris."

"But lunch ..."

"Okay. But someplace I can get a burger."

Driving home we felt refreshed, stronger.

The dogs — Mutz plus the visiting puppy — met us at the door. It was only eight-thirty. We'd been gone just over two hours.

"Where is everyone?"

"Don't ask," Gerry said. "Let's just sneak off to bed."

They found us before we got our coats off.

"We ordered pizza," Leslie said defiantly. "We pooled our money."

"Good."

Gabby handed me her Christmas list.

She: I'm sorry I was so bitchy this morning.

Me: Yes, you acted like a spoiled baby.

She: Well, I'm sorry.

Me: Okay. But I still think it's a good idea to make your own lunch.

She: No, that's okay. You can do it.

Me: No, really. I think it would be best …

Gerry and I eventually headed off to bed. Before turning out the light, I read the Christmas list. It included a request for a car, a trip to Toronto and/or Mt. Washington, a Nike sweatshirt, press-on nails, a professional massage, a six-pack of Kokanee, a pack of Player's Filter, a pink lighter and a joint. The last three items, Gabby noted, would fit in her stocking.

I chose to believe the list was our daughter's attempt at humour.

GIRLS AROUND THE HOUSE

ONE OF THE GIRLS SAYS: "WE WANT A NEW RULE. ANY TIME we're not home and a boy phones but doesn't leave his name? This is the rule: Do Star 69 and get the number. Then we'll know who it is."

I don't remember for sure which girl said this — the blue one, the orange one, the yellow one, the black one. Gabby or Lee; the eighteen- or the seventeen-year-old. Their hair colour changes, almost daily. If I were still kissing them goodnight I'd get confused: Who is who? I've *been* confused; sometimes it's not them in their beds. Weekend mornings I do a shoe check. If the Adidas running shoes and the black platform running shoes are in the mud room, then I'm okay, I know the girls are downstairs. But sometimes their shoes aren't there and I find strange shoes, alarmingly huge shoes, shoes no girl could ever fit into. Then I go snooping, the pitter-patter in my chest becoming boom, boom, boom.

I've found unknown boys sleeping alone beneath the girls' plaid flannelette quilt covers. Somebody this, somebody that, new friends of Leslie's over from Vancouver for the weekend, rock stars in embryo here for a gig.

I've found Gabby's best friend in bed with a boy, his hairy arm hanging over the side of the single bed and four jeans-covered legs poking out from beneath the quilt. I've found the vaguely known and the well-known friends of the girls asleep on the bedroom floor.

I tell Gerry, "At least the kids are safe. And we pretty well know whose house the girls are at. And what does it matter whose kids we've got? We're a community of parents. It's like all of us are raising these kids together."

"Only if they leave my bacon alone," Gerry says.

But the thing is, it's understood: We don't feed these overnight visitors. There's no whipping through a dozen eggs on a Sunday morning. I take this as a victory of sorts. Somehow a message has gotten through: This isn't a total flop house.

Possibly, Gerry is due all the credit. While I was away for two months last summer touring with my books, he got tough. I'd get stern, cryptic emails from him: "Caught #1 in our shower with his girlfriend. Told him this isn't a bordello. Told him if he uses our bathroom again, he'll be missing some vital parts."

I was touched by the way my husband assigned the kids numbers: #1, #2, #3, as in "#2 is being a dickhead"; "#3 didn't come home last night."

Weekly, I'd get longer reports that had a *Celestine Prophecy* tone to them. My husband had reached the top of the domestic mountain and now, in a revelatory flash, he finally understood juice consumption: "Did you know they drink a can of frozen concentrate a day?!"

When I returned home Leslie said proudly, "Have you

noticed how clean I keep the kitchen now? I had to, or that ox sitting out on the deck would go ballistic. If I so much as left a glass sitting on the counter, he'd follow me around hollering until I put it in the dishwasher. It was unnerving." He'd become an expert with a can of Comet.

And apparently Gerry had harassed him so much about using his razor that Leslie had actually gone out and bought his own. This is Progress, I'm certain of it.

Still, when you have kids, you also have their friends.

How many ways are there to split a baked potato? This isn't a joke. There have been times I've cut five baked potatoes into twenty-one portions to allow for the two extra people at the dinner table.

But sometimes we say no.

Last Sunday there were two boys downstairs playing Nintendo with the girls. I'd cooked a pot roast. Pot-roast smell hung in the air, heavy as smoke.

#2 came up and said: "I'm not that hungry."

"Okay."

"We're going out in a while for coffee."

"Okay."

"So I won't be eating much."

"Okay."

"So there'd be enough for Jeremy and Jeff."

"No."

"But I won't eat that much."

"Not tonight."

Twenty minutes later I called: "Dinner!" And, of course, #2 filled her plate, declaring: "I'm starving. I've only had a bagel all day."

You wonder about their short-term memory. You wonder what they think about *ours*.

The phone rings. The girls are out so I answer it. It's a boy for #3 who declines to leave his name. I run for a phone that has touch-tone capability so I can punch in Star 69. But before I get there the phone rings again. Suddenly I'm in a waking nightmare; I'm having a panic attack, my heart's racing.

The second call is from BC Tel asking how we like the service. I'm curt. "Fine! The service is fine!" I'm near shouting, exasperated because I've failed to get the boy's number.

My husband looks up from reading the Canadian Tire catalogue and says dryly, "You're over-involved. What do you care what boy is calling? They're *all* idiots."

Yes. But ...

When I was sixteen, the main excitement about returning home was asking, "Did anyone phone?" I made my mother keep a list. I'd grill her if she failed to get the name of a boy caller: "What did he *sound* like? Cute? Or icky?"

Now I realize that she probably did some editing like I do: If a boy leaves his name and I don't like that boy ... Short-term memory loss. It must be a female thing.

#2 has her sights set on a new boy. She asks, "How long did it take you to catch Dad?"

Without hesitation I say, "Six months."

"Six months!"

"I had obstacles. He was already married."

#2 knows this story: It was a bad marriage, there were no kids, her future Dad was ready to leave.

"Still," I said, "you can't rush these things. It's possible to make a wrong move, appear too eager. You never want to seem too available."

"It's been three weeks so far with me," #2 sighs. "But he's hanging out with us a lot and I've caught him looking at me when he thinks I'm not noticing."

"A good sign," I tell her. "When they start gazing at you with that perplexed but delighted expression on their face, I'd say things are pointing in the right direction. But never rush them. They've got to think it's their decision, that being with you is their idea. Those ones are the keepers."

The story I tell about meeting Gerry goes like this: I hired him. He'd come for a job interview at the treatment centre where I had a supervisory position. He was a friend of a man I worked with. "There's this guy with a degree in psychology and he's working on the ferries," is how my co-worker broached the subject.

Gerry didn't do well in the interview; he was reticent, awkward and sat on his hands. And I didn't like the clothes he was wearing; I thought he looked like a hick: orange pullover sweater, green shirt, a three-quarter-length leather coat that looked Country and Western. Country and Western! When everyone was into Dylan and the Stones.

Apparently I didn't fare that well, either. "I thought you were one of the women that ran the place," Gerry later said. "You were so tough and pushy. I figured you for a ball-breaker with hairy armpits."

After the interview I said to my co-worker, "No dice."

But a week later we needed a relief worker and, at my co-worker's suggestion, I gave Gerry a call. A different man walked through the treatment-house door, a relaxed and handsome man wearing jeans and a jean jacket. My stomach lurched. I thought: Marlboro Man. He had this slow, comfortable way of walking. He had this wavy brown hair, these sleepy blue eyes — "bedroom eyes," my mother called them when she finally met him.

That first night as a relief worker he was sent outside to play with the kids. But he didn't play with them like a Big Kid, tearing around and overdoing it . Rather, he played it cool, played it like a man, sort of hung around the kids, chased them a little, but, overall, seemed bored. And when he came inside and spoke to me, what he had to say was, "So, what's the *real* work around here?"

And I said: "Mister, you are hired!"

The girls' preoccupation with boys is normal, I tell Gerry; I've come to accept this. In spite of trying to make them into Young Feminists by exhorting them to "Be independent! Think for yourselves! Resist sexist stereotypes!" Maybe these things will happen later on — some internal switches will get flipped and they'll become the strong, enlightened young women I've always hoped for.

In the meantime, they have the age-old focus: boys,

parties, hair, makeup, gossip. I was the same. At their age I kept a diary and there was not one word of depth in it — every tight, scribbled, exclamated line was about boys. You want a teenage girl to be focused? She is, completely, utterly. I don't know why we expect something different. I don't know why we continue to try and enlighten them *at this time*. We'd be further ahead taking out shares in hair gel.

Which goes on their colourful heads by the cupful. I buy the cheapest brand, a 400-millilitre jar from Shoppers Drug Mart with a translucent green substance called "Super Hold" that I often pry from the bathroom walls and floor. Gel application: Bend over, apply liberally, then whip your head back so that drops of congealed gel splatter everywhere. A jar of gel lasts only a week.

"Don't you remember what it was like living with girls?" I ask Gerry, who's fuming because his hairbrush has gone missing again. He has two sisters, one older, one younger.

"No," he says decisively, he doesn't remember but he's certain that his sisters were never such a trial.

He doesn't "remember," of course, because he was too busy being the passionate focus in other female households.

Still, in this later incarnation, he's taken to being "the Dad" quite well. When the girls started coming home late and climbing in their bedroom window — or, rather, when *boys* started climbing in their bedroom window — he was ready. It reminded me of the way he trained the dog to stay away from the garbage can. He hid in the bushes and jumped out screaming when she made her sneaky visit. The tactic worked, generally: The dog was shocked and terrified and will now only assail the garbage can if Gerry is reliably out of sight.

So, from the man who's stated publicly that child rearing is very similar to training dogs, came his solution to the boys-in-the-window problem. One particular two a.m., he started awake. "Did you hear that?" he said, shaking me. "Listen!"

I listened, hearing nothing.

But Gerry, inexplicably sniffing the air, pulled on his boxer shorts and crept downstairs.

Now I listened. It was over quickly. A slight scuffle, a yelp, a banged-shut window.

Returning to bed, breathless but triumphant, he said, "That'll fix his sorry ass!"

"What? What happened?"

"I caught him, Colin from down the road, halfway in the window. I went to grab him by the hair but these little fuckers don't have hair anymore, so I grabbed his shirt collar. And he kept saying, 'I already have a girl-friend, I just came over to visit.' 'It's two o'clock in the fucking morning, Colin,' I said. 'You're lucky I didn't kill you, breaking into the house.' And Colin's blabbering, 'Honest, I already have a girlfriend.' 'Well, go visit her,' I said, 'and get the fuck out of here before I call the police.' 'Okay, okay, but don't hurt me,' the kid's squealing. So I shoved him out the window. Managed to give him a good bonk on the head."

"What were the girls doing?"

"Hiding under their quilts."

We had need of Colin's father some time later. It was Lee's seventeenth birthday, and she'd asked if she could have a few friends over for a barbecue.

"How many? What sex?"

"Six or seven. Girls."

The barbecue part went well. Eleven girls out on the deck, eating hamburgers and chips, chattering, laughing. Gerry and I inside, toasting one another with a glass of wine. Offering congratulations: "We've reached another milestone," we said, shining our eyes upon each other. "We've made it through another year. #3's a year closer to turning nineteen." Fools. The tipoff should have been the sudden rush for the bathroom after supper, the hair and makeup frenzy, the escalating phone calls.

Looking out the kitchen window, I saw several boys arranging deck chairs on the back lawn, cases of beer at their sides. And then another wave of kids arrived. One strapping guy of twenty-two or so wandered into the kitchen and asked if he could put his beer in the fridge.

"No, you can't," I snapped. "There's no room." Then I added, "Sorry," thinking: Be nice. Don't inflame them. Don't get them so mad at you that they want to trash the place.

By eight-thirty there were over twenty kids on the back lawn.

"What's going on?" I managed to briefly corral #3. She was impatient. A party was happening!

I grabbed her by her shoulders, trying for eye contact. She was wearing ripped jeans and a grubby sweatshirt, but her hair and makeup were exquisite.

"What's happening?" I repeated.

"What do you mean?" Her eyes were glazed over with what I hoped was only excitement.

"The sudden crowd on the back lawn is what I mean."

"Oh, that crowd."

"What *other* crowd did you think I meant?"

Her "talking to Mom" voice kicked in then — reasonable but barely tolerant. "No, it's totally okay," she said. "Like, completely chill out. It'll be all right. You're over-reacting again. They won't be staying long."

"How long?"

"An hour. Please? It's my birthday."

Another wave of kids arrived. One carried a portable boom box.

Gerry and I looked at each another nervously. It was like ... Cormac McCarthy's *Blood Meridian*! There we were, a pair of helpless settlers alone in our covered wagon on the great wide plain with a roving band of psychopathic cowboys just beyond our patch of safety who couldn't wait to scalp and kill us.

We called for reinforcements.

We called Colin's dad, Simon. Our good, neighbourhood friend.

Simon, like us, was a child of the early 1970s. He'd once lived in a cave in New Mexico for eight months, meditating and getting high on peyote. Now he had four teenage kids and worked in construction. We spoke the same language.

My idea was this: That the boozing kids on the lawn would look up and see this heavy-duty gathering of adult *men* drinking wine and listening to really cool blues, and they'd be awed and humbled before the way-cooler dominant males and behave themselves. Something like that.

"What did Simon say when you called him?"

"Said he'd be right over."

Simon arrived minutes later with his middle-aged hippie friend Marty.

"Hey, man," Simon said, "we were just on our way to a BB King concert. Had just toked up and were heading out the door. But, hey, my good friends and neighbours call needing help and I'm right there. That's what community is about, man. Helping one another in times of need. Right?"

"Right," we said, deeply grateful that he'd come, though Marty looked a touch disappointed about missing the concert. He looked a touch spaced-out, too, but I was relieved to see that he a was tall, heavyset man, and rough-looking, as if he'd like nothing better than to crunch a few skulls *for fun*. He definitely added menace and weight to the adult gathering. I was hoping that the combined and probably fictional reputations of Marty, Simon and my husband would cause the potential assassins on the back lawn to cower: "Fuck, man, don't mess with those old guys, they're crazy."

Simon took a long glance outside, waved at the crowd — which was arranged in a sedate circle talking and drinking and actually looking like a group of middle-aged suburbanites — and told us, "It's cool, man. I'm not getting any bad vibes. There won't be any trouble."

The baldheaded Colin was out there, too. He looked at his friend in alarm. What his lips seemed to say was: "Oh shit, my old man's here."

The whole scene now reminded me of a TV episode of *Nova*: "Gorillas in the Wild." The male gorillas arching their backs and pounding their chests in a display of male dominance. Only here it was Simon, Marty and Gerry dancing on the living-room rug to James Brown's "Get On Down" played at warp speed. Arching their backs, pounding their chests, *in a manner of speaking*. With the cranky young pretenders on the back lawn banished to the margins.

The next day Gerry had a terrible hangover. Maintaining the dominant male position at Lee's party had cost him dearly. At four o'clock he rolled off the bed and put on his coat. "I've got to go out," he said dismally. "I've got to have a Big Mac and a chocolate shake or I'm not going to make it."

"Guess what?" I said. "There'll come a time when you won't have to do this anymore. You won't have to be the dominant male." I was struck by the image, and continued. "The girls will be gone and you'll be the old, toothless, hairless male with nothing left to growl at."

"Why do you say these things? You like seeing me hungover, don't you?"

Nana joined us at the front door. She'd missed last night's party. By the time the bridge game was over at the Silver Threads at ten, the kids had moved on.

"What happened to him?" she asked, sounding delighted.

"He had too much fun last night defending his turf," I said.

"What you mean," Nana said, "was that he didn't know when to quit."

"What she means," my husband groaned, "was that I couldn't quit. It was a life-or-death situation. We had to keep the enemy at bay."

"I never know what he's talking about," Nana said.

I offered an explanation: "It's got to do with the girls, and having all these boys around. Because having girls around the house means having boys around the house, too."

"I know that," Nana said.

"Well," I continued, as Gerry drove off in his truck, "all these boys that are hanging around are putting us on the cusp, so to speak, pushing us over the edge. Because from here on in it's the scary slide, the old dust to dust rehearsal. And we don't like it. You understand what I'm saying? Those boys are making us old."

"I never know what you're talking about either," Nana said. "What makes me old is looking in the girls' bedroom. I don't know how you can stand it. All that mess. Make them clean it up!"

"So much cleaning, so little time ..." I said.

"What?"

"Yes, good idea. I'll get them to clean up their room. In fact, they can clean their way through adolescence. And I won't stop at their room. I'll move on to the laundry room, the kitchen walls, the yard, the world. It's worked in other generations. Why not in this one?"

"Now you're talking," my mother-in-law said. "Now you're finally making sense."

PROTEST

SEVERAL TIMES A DAY NANA VENTURES UP FROM HER downstairs suite. Her suite is her refuge from the upstairs world where our lives are seen by her as dizzying, chaotic. She often says with deep conviction, "I'm glad I'm not raising kids anymore. I don't remember it being so noisy."

She's referring, of course, to the music. But the music has little to do with raising kids. Or maybe it does. Because it's *our* music — Acid Jazz, House, Techno — and it's the major ingredient in that feel-good, satisfying place where we shelter on Friday nights.

"The thing about living with your mother," Gerry states, "is that you can still indulge in rebellion. Even though the world regards you as middle-aged and responsible. Particularly if you're inflicted with this label."

Protest nostalgia, I call it. It'll surface in future boomer retirement homes. There'll be recreational protest marches on Tuesday afternoons with a bunch of arthritic inmates dressed up like hippies and shuffling around an activity room carrying placards that say "Peace" or "Ban the Bomb," and everyone will be made to listen to Joan

Baez whining "We Shall Overcome." Only there won't be any drugs supplied — no marijuana, no acid — and free love will be as quaint a concept as decorating with macramé wall hangings. But the real hell will be having to go through the sixties again, straight. Having to go through an *idea* of it, rather, like an endless rerun of a bad sitcom, the bunch of us old and wrecked, and professionally kind attendants in white uniforms cheering from the sidelines: "C'mon, everybody! You look so cute! Let's really hear it for the Anti-Nuclear Rally!"

Some might say it's the end we deserve.

Concerning protest, my first husband — half of that fleeting, four-month marriage in 1970 — wrote on the marriage application form in the space reserved for "Religion": Protestant, in the sense that I protest.

I was nineteen years old, bored with university and impressed. Until three weeks later when I read the same line in a book by Lawrence Durrell.

My father was right: "Marion, shouldn't you get to know a man a little longer than two weeks before you marry him?"

Good point.

I belatedly took his advice and lived with Gerry for four years before we married. Not that this is what my father had in mind either. But I wanted to be sure; I scoured my future husband's mind like a coal miner, searching for hidden veins of Lawrence Durrell.

On our wedding day we left Leslie, our infant son,

with a sitter and got married at the local church, with just my sister and brother-in-law as witnesses. Afterwards, we had to cut short the celebration lunch because my breasts were leaking; the baby needed feeding.

Fast-forward twenty-odd years and it's another Friday night. The kids are out and upstairs it's rocking. It's that protest thing again: You can't really *hear* the music unless the volume's cranked, we tell each other. And, yes, we also say, our generation may be half deaf, but man, can we ever groove!

So it's Acid Jazz on the occasional Friday night. And friends over for wine, cheese and baguettes, music, talk.

Sometimes during these evenings Nana briefly joins us for a glass of wine. She tries listening to the music. "It's interesting," she'll say thoughtfully, in front of the guests. Or, with seemingly deep consideration: "That sounds like a door banging. Is that part of the music?" But most times she calls the pounding bass-driven beat, "That dreadful boom boom boom" and says, "I think you play it to annoy me."

"No," we say, "we love it!" And she shakes her head in disgust and retreats to her suite below.

We only turn up the volume now and then, giving one another assurances that we're not complete insensitives. But it's a difficult line, a difficult balance to maintain: consideration for Nana's elderly years alongside our desire — our need! — to play.

My mother-in-law gets her revenge during the week, though. I'll be working away in exquisite silence in my office and suddenly become aware of her music throbbing through the floorboards: Liberace at Las Vegas or

Harry Connick Jr. singing "When the Swallows Sang in Berkley Square."

She's lived downstairs for sixteen years. Her bedroom is directly beneath ours. "What? Are you crazy!" shrieked a holistic doctor I once consulted about warts, slapping his knee. (They want to know your *whole* life.) "Your mother-in-law sleeping in the room below you!"

He couldn't get over it; this was evidently one for the seminar circuit. He told me a mother-in-law joke. "A pharmacist tells a customer: In order to buy arsenic you need a legal prescription. A picture of your mother-in-law just isn't enough."

The problem is one of house design. We have our bedroom upstairs in what was supposed to be the Family Room; Nana's suite occupies part of the downstairs area originally designated as Master Bedroom. It's become a quaint and remote concept — Master Bedroom. When I see the bedroom fortresses of our friends and relatives, complete with their own bathrooms and walk-in closets, I can only marvel. What do couples do in there with all that space and privacy? Have full-throated, exuberant sex? Meditate? Have deeply felt, stimulating discussions free from interruptions?

Our bedroom is part of a top-floor "open plan," a design favoured by builders in the late 1970s. What were we thinking when we chose the design? What insanity possessed us to want everyone living together in one large room? Everything and everyone accessible. No quiet corners. No hideouts. It was a reckless gesture, decided upon when there was just one new baby. We had no idea how these babies expand — how they grow, along with their paraphernalia, to fill every corner of the house, unless kept in check, kept in separate rooms. During those early days of "open-plan" living I dreamed of having a playroom that was somewhere else — downstairs, outside, in another city — when, in fact, what we had was a playroom that included our bed and the kitchen floor and everything in between.

Nostalgia was part of it, too. As if the house design could ensure family closeness. As if with an "open plan" we would all hunker down together in perfect solidarity like some robust, mythical farm family from early in the century.

This farm-family image seduced many young mothers in the 1970s and '80s. A weird, back-to-basics mentality took over, many of us becoming evangelists for some bygone domestic Golden Age. Within a year of Leslie's birth I went from being an independent, semi-professional woman to a kind of retro farm woman — without the farm. Suddenly everything store-bought was suspect — food, cleaning products, anything produced by a corporation. And the only virtuous, moral, right-thinking, healthful, planet-saving, anti-corporate thing to do was to "go Natural," meaning we'd make everything ourselves — food, clothes, candles, compost. Some extremists even made their own soap and sanitary napkins. Our heroes at the time were an earnest young couple giving interviews on CBC-Radio: "Yes, it's true," they told their rapt audience, "we recycle everything. After a whole year all we've got are two cups full of garbage!"

Looking back, all this was the natural outcome of a certain generation that had settled down. Finished with protest marches and the freewheeling life, we looked around and said: "Okay, now what do we do?"

With me the Natural Affliction first surfaced around bread. The denatured, caramelized, wholewheat bakery bread that had sustained life for years was now dangerous, even life threatening. In my pursuit of purity I scoured the city until I found a supply of real wheat. Then I ground the wheat in my new wood-framed wheat grinder, which I bought, at considerable expense, from the Mormon Church, an organization with a survivalist bent; each Mormon family has a year's supply of food on hand — natural food, of course — in case of disaster, chaos and/or the breakdown of civilization as we know it. My wheat grinding friends and I were convinced that this breakdown was inevitable. Singing along at one of our herb tea and banana loaf gatherings with Jackson Browne's "After the Deluge," everyone was so *moved*.

But making the actual bread wasn't that easy; there was the awful problem of yeast. I just couldn't get the bread to rise.

"But you hate cooking!" my mother reminded me when I asked for help. She was from the generation that loves labour-saving devices, instant food and lethal cleaning products. She was confused by my transformation. "Why would you want all that work?" she asked, amazed. "Your grandmother had all that work but she had no choice. There was no such thing as Instant

Rice or Frozen Pizza in those days. She made everything from scratch and even boiled water on a wood stove to do her washing. She was a wreck! She never had a minute to herself."

Yes! Yes! I remember chanting with lust and envy. A wood stove! Everything from scratch!

My mother had no desire to bake bread herself, she told me, but if I really needed to, why not look for a book in the public library? She was clearly amused at my newfound domestic zeal and I took affront. "No! No! I'm not laughing at you," she assured me. "Baking bread and turning into a old-fashioned homemaker is so much better than when you were a hippie and going to all those protests and living in that filthy hovel."

I was deaf to her entreaties to return to the instant world, though, and happily increased my workload a hundredfold. On one occasion, I spent six hours with forty pounds of apples and managed to produce, at one-thirty in the morning, three minute jars of jelly. Sweating, hauling, measuring, boiling, while the babies and my husband slept.

"The jelly's beautiful!" I told myself, admiring the cloudy and not quite golden colour of my labours. And it's true, I hoarded those jars of jelly like trophies. We had them for years, until the mould finally claimed them.

Possibly, this back-to-basics mania was involved in my enthusiasm to have my mother-in-law live with us. At the time, I was reading a book called *Preserving Summer's Bounty* by Marilyn Kluger. Alongside directions for fruit and vegetable canning , pickle making and home drying, were wonderful vignettes about family life on the farm in the 1930s. Chapter titles included "Grandmother's Mincemeat," "Grandpa's Outdoor Cellars" and "Preserving Fruits in Spirituous Liquids." I rhapsodized over sentences like this: "The kitchen table was a veritable cornucopia for the harvest; in the centre, piled in a crunchy mound on the ironstone meat platter, might be quail Dad had hunted, or smoky fried ham slices cut from the muslin-shrouded ham hung in the smokehouse."

Enthralled by these images, I pictured deliriously happy family scenes: Nana and I with our sleeves pushed up, faces sweaty, and possibly wearing kerchiefs, stirring gallons of apple butter over an outside firepit, the children racing about in their rustic, homemade clothes, Gerry in a red-and-black felt shirt, lustily chopping wood for the fire. A dog or two cavorting alongside the free-range chickens and the rows of late-sprouting potatoes.

Not to be, of course. The kids wanted spandex. My husband wanted TV football. And Nana wanted independence. Meaning, she was done with full-time domesticity. Now she intended to enjoy life, she said, play bridge several times a week and travel.

This is when I discovered the word "baffle." Being able to baffle, I decided, is another way to protest: You're protesting the *idea* people have of you.

Our friends were baffled that we'd allow a parent to live with us. They offered us mother-in-law jokes like sympathy cards:

    — My mother-in-law was bitten by a dog yesterday.

    — How is she now?

    — She's fine. But the dog died.

I was baffled when I realized that Nana wasn't the babushka-wearing, rocking-chair user of my fantasies, that she was, rather, a modern, travelling grandma with plans of her own. (For years, our kids thought that Nana owned the airport because she was always rushing off to catch her plane.)

Gerry was baffled then nervous when I abandoned my wholewheat mania in favour of another mania — writing.

"Something's got to go," I told him, "and it's the bread. And the canned rosehips and the jellies and the tomato seedlings. Do you realize how much time these things take?"

As a family, we continue to baffle one another. It's become a major family trait. It's like we're constantly saying to each other, "Aha! You thought you knew me but you're wrong. I'm liable to do wonderful, strange and unexpected things. And you'll never know what my next baffling move will be!"

Which brings me back to my mother-in-law, a master of the subtle protest. What's she protesting? Her widowhood? Her age? The raucous music above her? There's got to be some explanation for her almost nightly visits to our bedroom. *Almost* nightly. But that's the brilliance of it, the baffling, random, protesting brilliance.

Our bedroom door is actually a bifold, which means that it can't be locked, that even the cat can nudge it open. Everyone, but especially Nana, feels free to enter at any time.

Now and then Gerry and I complain about this to each other.

Him: It's insane. Why don't we put in a real door with a lock?

Me: How much would that cost?

Him: A fair whack. And then the open plan would be destroyed.

Me: About time it was destroyed.

Him: Well, I don't know. What about market value? (This from a man who doesn't like to hammer in nails because that's too much of a commitment; he always leaves a quarter of an inch sticking out — "In case I change my mind.")

So the bifold door has become a sixteen-year-old temporary solution.

We'll be lying in bed at night, reading or watching TV or doing other things, and hear Nana's groans as she mounts the basement stairs. Then we'll hear the determined flap of her tread as she makes her way through the living room towards our bedroom. We brace ourselves, then cover up or fling ourselves to opposite sides of the bed.

She's usually clutching the daily paper when she enters, the paper we've already read.

"Thought you might want this," she says, sitting herself with difficulty on the edge of the bed, a futon.

I know she's just wanting company, a few minutes' chat, some human contact — which is why we've hesitated in speaking to her directly.

I mentioned the problem to my sister-in-law, who was visiting from Toronto. "It's practically every night!" I whined.

"What you need to do," Karen advised, "is as soon as you hear her coming, pull off your pants and jump on each other. If she walks in on that, she'll never do it again."

What immediately came to mind was a bondage scene: whips, chains, goat mask.

I told Gerry. "Do you think her blood pressure could stand it?" I asked, a question he answered with, "So which one of us would do the whipping?" His sudden interest was disconcerting.

But we considered Karen's advice.

It was after a Friday night of wine and Acid Jazz. The kids were out and his mother was, we hoped, safely below. We could hear her TV set droning away beneath us. There was a "now's our chance" look in my husband's eyes.

Pulling off his jeans at the side of the bed, he suddenly screamed out: "Wow! Oh! Oh! Oh! Give it to me, baby!"

"A little ahead of yourself, aren't you?"

But he continued in this vein. It was almost shocking; I'd never heard him talk like this.

He moved to the bedroom window, hanging his head out and shouting at his mother's window directly below: "Umm. Yes! More! More! Ah, it's so gooooood!"

"The neighbours!"

"Yes! Yes! The neighbours. Let's invite the neighbours,

too!" He turned to me, still yelling, wild-eyed and na-
ked except for his black socks.

I shut the window.

But my husband kept it up, pacing, directing his shouting at the bedroom floor. "We love to do it in this house.
Love it! Love it! We do it all the time. Any chance we
get. In the bathroom! Under the kitchen table! Under
the Christmas tree! On the dining-room table! In the
car! Ummmm! Yes! We never stop. We do it all the time.
We can't get enough. Everything excites us! The paper-
boy! The Thanksgiving turkey! The fifteen pairs of shoes
blocking the mud-room door! The organic vegetables
going mouldy in the fridge! The tins of cat food in the
pantry! We do it in the pantry! We do it outside on top
of the garbage cans. And on the deck beside the old
barbecue. We do it on the pile of grass clippings up by
the road. Oh, it's such a turn-on. Ummm! Ummm! Everywhere! There's no stopping us."

He paused, panting, and fell on the bed, worn out.

Nana's only remark the next morning was disconcerting; she thought it was our music. "All that yelling about
barbecues and garbage cans! You call that music?"

"Well, yes, in a strange way, we do," Gerry said.

"You mean you actually pay money to buy that so-
called music?" she continued, incredulous.

"Yes, yes we do."

It was beyond her. "You must be out of your minds,"
she declared.

"That too," her son answered, smiling, pleased at the
thought. "It's absolutely true. We're out of our minds."

Deep in the Tennessee hills, a farmer's mule kicked his mother-in-law to death. An enormous crowd of men turned out for the funeral. The minister, examining the crowd outside the church, commented to a farmer friend, "This old lady must have been mighty popular. Just look how many people left their work to come to her funeral."

"They're not here for the funeral," snickered the friend. "They're here to buy the mule."

This is a joke my mother-in-law snipped out of *Readers Digest* and gave to me a few weeks after she moved in all those years ago.

"Just so you don't get any ideas," she told me, and we laughed.

It's baffling. We just keep on laughing.

TIC-TAC-DOE

BECAUSE WE COULDN'T SELL OUR 1980 PEUGEOT — IT HAD a blown head gasket — I phoned a number in an ad in the community paper: *Tic-Tac-Doe Cabinets. Will trade kitchen cabinets for something of value.* I told the man on the line that what we wanted were bathroom cabinets and the area around the tub tiled. If he could do this we would give him the car.

"All it needs is a head gasket," I said. "And it's in beautiful shape. The body's great, a dark wine colour. It's got a plush interior and a sun roof. It looks like a Mercedes."

He said he was interested and we arranged a time for him to come and look at the job.

"What's your name?" I asked.

"Tickner. Daryl Tickner."

Two nights later Daryl Tickner drove up in a 1972 Plymouth, beige in colour, with large patches of rust around the rear wheels. A man in his late thirties, tall but solidly built, wearing black cowboy boots. He had a long, thin ponytail that hung over his plaid jacket. The jacket was dirty with smears of oil on the sleeves and chest. He wore a diamond stud in his left ear.

He took off his boots when he came in the house. Then looked at the bathroom. The sink area consisted of a platform of white melamine board, a curtain (green and yellow flowers) hung in place of cabinet drawers, and the floor was covered in lime green tiles, a colour that for some reason I had loved deeply in 1984. To complete the sordid effect, the sheeting around the bathtub was cracked and warped; black mould was growing around the edges.

Of this Daryl said, "It'll have to be replaced before we can put on tile. I'll have to rip it out and put up half-inch plywood first." He sounded disgusted.

He put his boots back on and went outside with Gerry to look at the car. It had been sitting in the driveway for a year and a half and one of the rear tires was flat. Daryl opened a front door and peered inside the car. Then he looked under the hood. It was impossible to guess what he was thinking.

I watched the men from the vestibule window. They walked solemnly around the car several times, then leaned against the hood and had a smoke.

Then they came inside. This time Daryl left his boots on.

"Nothing else wrong with the car besides the head gasket?" he asked.

"No."

"Alright," he said, "I'll do it, but I'll need three hundred dollars for materials. I've got to get the cabinet top and the wood to build the cabinets. I'll trade my labour for the car. You pick up the tile you want for the tub. Soon as we get that, I'll have my partner out here laying her up."

He wanted the three hundred dollars up front. We balked.

"I can't be putting out money like that," he said, "what with a family to feed."

"A family to feed, yes, of course," we said anxiously. And agreed to his terms. How much longer would the car sit in the driveway unless we did? How much longer would the rot and mould around the bathtub continue to disgrace us?

Before we gave him the money, though, we wanted a reference.

"No problem," Daryl said. And gave us the name and phone number of a Dr. Donnelly. "I put in his kitchen. Call him tonight if you want."

It was a Monday night.

"You get the tile by the weekend and the cash to me tomorrow morning and we can sign the contract. The bathroom will be finished this time next week. But I don't work Sunday," he added. "I never work on the Lord's day."

After Daryl left, I found the number of Dr. Donnelly in the phone book. He was listed at a clinic on the other side of town. His phone number was different from the one Daryl gave us — probably his home phone, I reasoned. Gerry did the phoning. He was grinning when he finished the call. "Dr. Donnelly says Daryl doesn't have hemorrhoids. And he said he did the work okay; there weren't any problems."

"So there really is a Dr. Donnelly?"

"Must be. He's in the book."

"Good," I said. "I'm sure Daryl needs the work. And if he's hooked into a church …"

"That's the oldest con in the book," Gerry said. "Guys talking about the Lord. That's what sucks people in. Especially old people. They think it means reliable, honest, trustworthy. Pretty soon they're having their roofs redone or their houses painted when they don't need it. And then it's thousands of dollars later. All because of a line about the Lord. I knew a guy called Ray who did this all the time. With him it was septic tanks. Digging them up for nothing."

But we went ahead with the deal.

The next morning I drove the forty miles to Daryl's house. It was ten-thirty when I got there. A shabby house, white with light blue trim, at the end of a cul-de-sac. Two rusted cars in the driveway. An old blue pickup truck parked outside on the road.

After several minutes a man answered the door. Late forties, skinny, in his undershirt, unshaven.

"Sorry, I was asleep. Didn't hear the bell."

He asked me in.

"Daryl's out back. I'll get him."

"This is my partner Ray," Daryl said, introducing me to the man when he came in. "Ray Tacowski — the 'Tac' of Tic-Tac-Doe." Tattoos of snakes on both of Ray's forearms. I noticed that most of Daryl's bottom teeth were missing.

We sat at the kitchen table. Ray had disappeared. There were children's drawings tacked on the wall, and more drawings and notices on the fridge door. On the kitchen counter were several boxes of breakfast cereal lined up neatly, a jar of instant coffee, a jar of Coffee-mate. Looking into the dining room I could see a china cabinet filled with crystal wine glasses, china plates, cups and saucers. The place looked reassuring, like an established household.

Everything was businesslike. Daryl had a contract ready for me to sign. With a clause that said the contract was void if the work wasn't completed within thirty days.

He showed me plans for someone else's kitchen. "Doing cabinets in exchange for a motorhome," he said, "but I'll do your bathroom first."

I gave him six fifty-dollar bills. He gave me a receipt.

"I'll be out tomorrow to take measurements," he said.

"What time?"

"After supper."

Later I told my husband: "I met the 'Tac' of Tic-Tac-Doe Cabinets. Ray Tacowski. Wonder if it's the same Ray you knew?"

"Fat guy? Bald?"

"No. He's skinny, got hair. Brown and greasy."

"Doesn't sound like the same Ray."

"Looks like an alcoholic. Shakes when he walks."

"Figures. They're both probably on step one of a nineteen-step recovery program."

"Could be," I said. "Which is why we've got to hang in there. People in recovery programs need our support."

"Mmmm."

"Anyway, they've got the money now."

"You didn't give them cash, did you?"

"That's what he wanted."

"Jesus."

"What difference would a cheque make now? We're already committed. It'll be all right, you'll see. His house didn't look fly-by-night. It looked like a place where people lived."

"So what? You think crooks don't live in houses?"

"If you're so worried why'd you agree to the deal?"

"Because it's the only way we'll get rid of the car," Gerry said.

That night we drove into town. We spent two hundred dollars on five boxes of white tile, a fifty-pound sack of mortar, a tub of grout and a new toilet seat.

Gerry stacked the materials on the front porch.

We saw Daryl three days later, Friday night.

"Jeez, sorry about the last few days," he said. "My son's been sick. I couldn't go anywhere."

We said we understood.

He took the bathroom measurements.

"What colour countertop?" he asked.

"White."

"I'll have to order it. You wouldn't want pink, would you? I've got some real nice pink."

"No," we said, "we want white."

A week later I phoned Daryl.

"Where have you been?"

"Jeez, I should have phoned. I got the flu. I been so sick I couldn't get out of bed. It's really put me behind. Remember I told you about my son being sick? I got it from him. Last night I had a temperature of one hundred and three."

I said I understood. And hoped he'd get well.

Another week went by.

"I keep trying to go to work," Daryl said when I phoned again, "but this bug's really laid me out. I've had to cancel the motorhome deal. All I do is sleep. But I've ordered the countertop. Should be here next week."

When I told Gerry, he said, "Flu, my ass. He's stalling till the thirty days are up on the contract. Then the deal will fall through. He'll have the three hundred bucks and we'll have dick. And just try to get the money back from him then. I know these guys. This is the way they operate."

"I wonder if Dr. Donnelly is the 'Doe' of Tic-Tac-Doe Cabinets?" I said. Picturing another guy like Daryl and Ray — the janitor, maybe, at Dr. Donnelly's office. With the name of Don. Hanging around waiting for the call from pigeons like us. Picturing a Three Stooges trio with a sinister twist.

I called Daryl twice the following week. The first time he told me the countertop had come in and that he'd been working on the cabinets. "But the damnedest thing happened today," he said. "A bearing on my saw broke. If I can't fix it I'll have to get a new saw."

The other call was ten a.m. on a Saturday morning.

A woman answered the phone. When I asked for Daryl she said, "He's in bed."

I started to tell her why I was calling: "It's about the cabinets … I was wondering if he's bringing them out today."

"Just a minute," she said, sounding annoyed, and went and got him.

"Yeah, they're just about finished," Daryl said when he finally got on the line. "I'll bring them out on Monday and we can wrap the whole job up in two days."

It was eight days later, on a Sunday, that we saw Daryl. After several more calls from me he said he could see I was getting antsy. "I don't usually work on the Lord's day," he said, "but for you I'll make an exception; I'll come out after church and we'll get started."

"What time will that be?"

"After lunch. But I don't have the cabinets together," he said.

"Bring the countertop anyway," I said, thinking we'd at least have something to show for our money.

At three he drove up.

"Sorry I'm late," he said, "but the damnedest thing happened. I was getting gas beside the Waddling Dog Inn and who should I bump into but my lawyer. So we went and had a beer. Haven't seen him in a coon's age."

The countertop was in the back seat of his car. White. It looked okay. He stopped when he was carrying it into the house to have a look at the tile on the front porch. "That's the tile, eh?" he said. And sighed.

Then he got to work tearing the bathroom apart. He pulled the sheeting away from the tub. "Look at that," he said, almost delighted. "You've got an ant's nest in there."

We put on the bathroom fan because the mildew smell was so bad. Moments later he asked me for a cold drink. Not long after this, Gerry asked me for a band-aid. He said Daryl had a rash on his hand that he wanted to cover.

The tearing apart, the sawing, the hauling drywall outside continued for an hour. I was making supper. Gerry was helping Daryl. Before long he came into the kitchen and said Daryl was sitting on the edge of the bathtub holding his jaw. "He's got a toothache."

Minutes later I met Daryl in the hallway. He looked miserable. His hand was still holding his jaw. "It's killing me," he said. "I've got to go."

I said I understood.

After he'd gone, Gerry said, "At least he's left his tools. He'll have to come back and finish the job now."

We looked at the tools: a wooden tool box, a battery-driven drill, a hand saw, tape measures, a level and three new hammers with the price tags still on — all $49.95.

"He probably bought those with our three hundred dollars," Gerry said.

He'd left his jacket, too, thrown on the bathroom floor.

The only problem was that now the bathroom was completely useless. Daryl had disconnected the bolts to the toilet and the bathtub was filled with mouldy debris from the walls. The pink insulation on the walls was exposed and the bathroom floor was splattered with used drywall mud. This meant we had to use the toilet in the basement.

"We paid three hundred dollars for some guy to come and trash our bathroom," Gerry said.

I left the sheets on the floor covering the route from the front door to the bathroom. Because I was certain we'd see Daryl the next day.

I should have known better: the toothache. He'd seen his dentist, he was on antibiotics, he'd had to stop four times on the drive home from our place because of the pain, the pain was so bad he could hardly see, he'd had a temperature of one hundred and three.

"What? one hundred and three again?" Gerry said.

"So maybe he's sickly," I said. "But he's trying. You can tell he's trying. He says he'll be out tomorrow for sure."

At eight-fifteen the next morning Daryl phoned: "I'll be out later this morning. I'm just finishing up the cabinets."

When Gerry phoned from work to see if Daryl had shown up I told him about the early call. "Eight-fifteen in the morning," I said, impressed.

"Up at eight-fifteen?" Gerry said. "He must have shit the bed."

At three-thirty I phoned Daryl.

"What happened?"

"You won't believe my day," he said. "But I won't bore you with the details. We'll get it done tomorrow. That's a promise."

That night Gerry said: "I'm going to phone him up, tell him to keep the three hundred dollars and I'll keep his tools. And I'll finish the goddamned bathroom myself."

I managed to calm him down. "Confrontation won't get us anywhere," I said. "And who's going to buy a bunch of tools, most of which are used? The only way we're going to get those cabinets is by playing along with him, waiting it out. We already have the countertop and we haven't signed over the car yet. If we just hang in there a little longer, I'm sure it will work out. He's obviously learning how to be reliable."

"This is just like social work," said my husband, who works with the behaviour problems at the local middle school.

Meanwhile there was the mildew smell coming from the bathroom. And the three a.m. treks downstairs in the dark to pee.

Two days later Daryl and Ray showed up with the cabinets. It was the first time Ray had been to the house. The delay in their arrival was because they'd had to borrow a truck. ("My brother's got my Aerostar.") It was six-thirty. I'd phoned their place at five. A kid had answered the phone. "No, he's not here, he'll be back in an hour."

"Is he delivering cabinets?" I asked, hoping I didn't sound too desperate. "Just a minute," the kid said. I heard a woman's voice in the background, then the kid told me uncertainly, "Yeah, he's delivering cabinets." I pictured Daryl sitting at his kitchen table and mouthing to the kid: "Tell her I'm not home." And eating his supper of canned spaghetti and beer and laughing.

So I was happy and relieved when they actually showed up. They carried the cabinet frames into the house, puffing and laughing. Ray was wearing a T-shirt that said "Crazy Gringo." "No doors or drawers yet," Daryl said happily, "but they're just about finished." They'd brought two sheets of plywood, as well, for nailing up around the tub, and left them propped against the house. They were in a good mood, pleasant, talkative. Proud of themselves, it seemed, for actually delivering the goods.

They stayed long enough to bring the cabinets into the hallway and tell us they'd be back tomorrow. Which, miraculously enough, they were, managing to work three straight hours and arriving only four hours later than they said. This day was their most productive; they nailed up the plywood and got the cabinets in place. I made them coffee, telling them I'd be back in fifteen minutes, I had to pick up my daughter from school. When we returned they were sitting inside the Peugeot. Daryl was in the driver's seat, his hands on the steering wheel. It looked like they were pretending they were driving somewhere.

After that, the pace picked up. Slightly. We got two more two-hour workdays out of them. When Daryl said they'd be out mid-morning, I blithely told Gerry that it would be mid-afternoon. And it was. Unloading the cabinet doors from his car trunk, Daryl said, "I've nearly had a nervous breakdown doing this job." And I said, "So have we!"

During these days Daryl and Ray laughed together

while they worked. And they had long conversations about the right way to hammer in the cabinets and even one about a woman who wore coke-bottle glasses: "You could dump a pot of potatoes over her head and she wouldn't know." Ray said, "Jeez, it'd blow my mind if I couldn't see." Daryl sang hymns while he worked: "Rock of Ages" and "Onward Christian Soldiers."

The toilet had been removed by now and sat on blocks on the front porch like an old car that would one day be worked on. Our toilet rudely exposed for the neighbours to see: its shocking white body, its sad, empty bowl. I recited to Gerry the first lines of a poem by Russell Edson: "The toilet slides into the living room on its track of slime demanding to be loved …"

I found myself happy to see Daryl and Ray when they'd finally arrive for their daily two hours. The bathroom was being worked on; something was happening. Ray turned out to be a talker; he told me to get rid of the English ivy in our yard because it was killing the pear tree. He said he'd been in the tree business for fifteen years (removing trees that didn't need removing?) and said he knew what he was talking about. When Ray wasn't telling me about his past businesses (trees, roofs, windows), sawing bits of plywood or cutting tiles, he was rolling cigarettes, playing tag with the dog or using the bathroom downstairs. He was polite but very nervous. I noticed that when he sat on the front porch smoking he couldn't keep his legs still; they shook of their own accord. But the work progressed. Daryl seemed quite moved and said "thank you" when I told him that the job was looking good.

But this pair of two-hour workdays turned out to be our Golden Age with Tic-Tac-Doe Cabinets. It's true Daryl and Ray finally got the tile on the walls, but it was clear they didn't know what they were doing. The tiles were placed crookedly, mortar was splattered on the ceiling, the bathtub, the floor. And many of the tiles were chipped. Neither of them, it appeared, knew about tile cutters; they'd broken over two dozen tiles trying to fit them around the faucets. And then they started grumbling loudly to each other about all the time the job was taking. "We're almost doing this for free," Daryl said, and Ray said, "Yeah, it's like doing a welfare job."

They never did grout the tile like they said they would; they simply didn't show up. Gerry finished the job. Grouting, hanging cupboard doors, replacing cracked tiles, replacing the toilet (it finally getting hugged by him on the return trip to the bathroom — oh happy toilet!) and cleaning up the appalling mess they'd left. Gerry figured he spent about nineteen hours all told. But the thing was, we still had their tools. Added to Daryl's collection were Ray's: another electric hand saw, three more hand drills, hammers, screwdrivers and an impressive assortment of nails. We also found Daryl's copy of our signed contract with him, and his rough sketch of our bathroom. We put everything in the trunk of the Peugeot, which, of course, still remained ours. While they were here they'd never once asked to start it up.

To finish the bathroom we bought some stick-on tiles for the floor, black and white, and two new black towels. The new toilet seat was installed and a new white shower curtain hung from a new chrome curtain rod. A coat of white semi-gloss paint was applied. The bathroom looked dazzling, even with the crooked tiles. We kept going in there just to marvel at the transformation, to gape and gasp; at last we had a bathroom where our guests would be proud to pee. The only thing missing was one of the doors beneath the sink; Daryl hadn't brought it with him on his last visit.

The final call to Daryl occurred over this issue. It was a Tuesday morning, two weeks after their botched tile job and a full three months after we'd signed the thirty-day contract.

Gerry told him we wanted the cabinet door. And asked Daryl when he planned to deliver it. But Daryl started complaining. He said he'd been misled (his word) about the job, and Gerry said that, as a contractor, Daryl should have known what he was getting into. Then Gerry mentioned the five hours it had taken him to do the grouting and Daryl said, "Bullshit, ask anybody in the trade, it's only a half-hour job." After this exchange, the "screw you's" and the "goddamns" started flying. Also these: "You're full of shit"; "Blow it out your ass"; and "Who the hell do you think you're talking to?" And then an angry Daryl saying he'd be right out with the door and my husband shouting, "The sooner the fucking better."

That was six months ago. We haven't heard from Daryl or Ray since. And we still have their tools. And the car. Everyone who visits us hears this story and then has a look at the tools in the back of the Peugeot. Estimates of their worth run anywhere from five hundred dollars to two thousand dollars, well in excess of the value of the car. Someone suggested that maybe they were stolen. And everyone gives us advise as to what we should do next: sell the tools at a garage sale; send Daryl and Ray a registered letter telling them that we're storing their tools at two dollars and fifty cents a day; phone up Dr. Donnelly and tell him to never again recommend Tic-Tac-Doe Cabinets; consult a lawyer. And about the tools: It's not unlikely that we'll have them with us for the next several years.

But it's the car that's really the problem: We can't seem to get rid of it. It clings to us like our forlorn toilet, demanding to be loved. It costs too much to fix, which is why we've been driving a 1979 Ford Fairmont for the last two years, ever since the Peugeot's head gasket blew on the Pat Bay Highway two days before Christmas. We don't think Daryl and Ray still have a claim on the car because they didn't fulfill the terms of the contract.

So really this story is one long classified ad: *Peugeot For Sale. Beautiful body; needs head gasket.* If anyone reading this is interested in owning the car, we'll let it go for two hundred dollars. Failing that, we have an idea for another ad: *WANTED: Door-to-door vacuum salespeople. Will trade valuable luxury car for state-of-the-art vacuum cleaner. Only the desperate need apply.*

HOLISTIC BALL OF WAX

GERRY AND I WERE HUDDLED IN BED LATE AT NIGHT HAVING another talk. I was in one of my agonizing moods.

Me: It's about the kids. I don't know. They seem so wild, so unfocused.

Him: What are you talking about? They're working, they're in school. They're always here. Wild is when you don't see them for weeks on end. We should be so lucky.

Me: Yes, but we don't seem able to control them.

Him: They're beyond control.

Me: Meaning?

Him: Look, the only control you have over teenagers is in your wallet. And in any relationships you were able to cement with them when they were younger, before puberty struck. After that, forget it.

Me: But I see other families.

Him: So what?

Me: They don't seem as raucous as ours. There are too many parties going on in this family and there's not enough quiet contemplation. Not enough reading or walks. The kids are having too much fun.

Him: Too much fun?

Me: Yes. Everyone's having too good a time. That's all they seem to live for — having a good time. I'm worried they won't be prepared for LIFE.

At this point Gerry let out an enormous sigh. "Give it a rest," he said. And then, sitting up on one elbow, added, "Agony's become a preferred state for you, hasn't it? If it's not about the kids, it's the writing."

"Preferred?"

"Yes. Of all the states available to you, you frequently pick agony. Why not joy? Or serenity? Here's one. Why not manic excitement? But you wouldn't like that, would you? You prefer anguish, despair, mental suffering. Agony is your middle name. You must really enjoy it."

"Are you trying some kind of reverse psychology on me?"

"You see? Already you're agonizing about my motives."

I tore off the covers and raced to the office for the Oxford dictionary. Returning to bed with a definition, I told my husband triumphantly, "Besides 'anguish', it says here 'paroxysms of pleasure'."

"Exactly. You love the crud you find at the bottom of the barrel."

True enough, though I've tried hard to not agonize about what I find there. And it's not agonizing exactly; it's more like worried curiosity — pulling apart, probing, delving, excavating. Digging around for essences, truth. Like what a dog does with its quarry.

But this isn't what Gerry means, the part of me that's the shut-away writer, writing. He means the other, ordinary me, the domestic self, the self that often gets drenched by the leftover slop of creative work, the self that indulges in ceaseless, pain-in-the-neck fussing about things beyond my control, like feeling bad about other people's lives or the sadistic whims of book reviewers. The constant worry about whether eating three eggs a week will eventually kill me.

The two sides.

The writer as Split Woman.

But I've come to like this split because, somehow, each side nourishes the other. And I've decided another thing about all this whining and fretting, all this lovely, real-life neuroticism: I like that, too.

There it is.

Don't tell the New Spiritualists.

As far as they're concerned, I'm unenlightened and badly evolved; higher self-awareness is hopelessly beyond me. Instead of being a rock in a stream and letting the flurry of life rush over me, I'm grabbing at the water like a drowning woman. I'm not partaking of life as a holistic ball of wax. I'm out of step with their times. Instead of living in the positive moment, I'm wallowing in life's negatives. As a result, I'm about as self-actualized as ... well ... everyone else. What a relief!

I'm getting tired of the New Spiritual Age. How did we ever get so hoodwinked, so duped? Do we really believe we're as shallow, as flat and boring, as the New Spiritualists proclaim?

Their constant exhortation to *Live in the Positive Mo-*

ment has become a new form of social tyranny, a spiritual and mental straitjacket. I'm convinced of it. Because the moment we're all supposed to be experiencing, according to the New Spiritualist entrepreneurs — a little dab of Buddhism and Native culture, a generous dab of free enterprise — is one that's relentlessly wonderful.

Not that I have anything against "wonderful." But all the time? What fresh oppression is this? I want to cry, paraphrasing Dorothy Parker in a vain attempt to sweep the New Spiritualists aside. Vain because they're everywhere now proclaiming their message through thousands of books, PBS specials, movies about the Dalai Lama and even a TV commercial in which a Buddhist-looking actor in an orange robe announces with a cosmic twinkle in his eye that REMAX helped him find his monastery at a really good price.

At parties complete strangers will engage me in earnest, ruthlessly positive Living in the Moment discussions about the most banal subjects. The weather! The living room they find themselves in! Their glazed eyes and trusting exclamations of wonderfulness *everywhere* remind me of cult members from the 1980s — blissed out and empty. I find myself longing to meet that sour-looking woman sitting by herself against the wall. She's the one I'm drawn to. It's like craving a fresh breath of negativism. Like longing for brooding solitude. ("Just go away, goddammit, and let me be miserable.")

A steady diet of positive moments can wear you out; we're not programmed for continual smiling. We need to furrow our brows and purse our lips now and then; we need to think deeply. Sometimes it's a relief to scowl.

And Living in the Positive Moment is such a nuisance. Right in the middle of a fabulous daydream you're supposed to holler at yourself to Pay Attention! Be Mindful! You're supposed to slap your own face and bring yourself back — to the traffic snarl, the dirty bathtub — the idea being that this is where "wonderful" can be found and if you just concentrate and study hard and buy the books and tapes and attend the retreats then all the crap in your life will be wonderful, too. But what I want to say is this: What's an imagination for if you can't leave the present tense now and then, if you can't imagine what the rest of humanity is experiencing, if you can't partake of all the junk of life, too, the nitty-gritty, the sludge at the bottom of the barrel.

And so I'm giving up this Eastern-flavoured spirituality. Trying to practise it has become, as we used to say, a drag. And I don't like the way it produces guilt in me. If I'm not adhering to the practices — stillness, mindfulness, egolessness — then I'm way down on the wisdom ladder, grossly formed, somehow unworthy, and definitely not wonderful.

All this fretting about Living in the Positive Moment came to a boil when I drew a line in the sand and declared myself, when I defected from the cause. I made a huge decision, as big a decision as the one I made when I threw out the black plastic compost bin and accompanying how-to video. Shocked friends accused me then of abandoning the Organic Age. "But that's what we do in these times," I snarled in reply. "We go about trying on 'ages' and then abandoning them like old coats. We're *shoppers*, that's what we are. So what? Isn't everyone greedy for the next new thing?"

What I did to mark my liberation from the New Spiritual Age was drop out of yoga class. A small, blundering gesture, to be sure — step one of a recovery program with "steps" stretching into infinity — but a clear beginning.

And dropping out felt … wonderful! I told my friend and yoga partner Rita, "I really miss sweating my brains out at the gym."

"You're quitting yoga?" she gasped.

"I can't do everything," I said weakly. "I can't do yoga and go to the gym. There isn't enough time. And I really love the treadmill."

"Well, now I know what to get you for your birthday," she replied. "Hamster feed."

But what bliss! No more lying on those cold plastic mats at the Sanscha Hall — breathing, stretching, freezing. Trying to stay sweetly calm. Even though Betty, the instructor, was amazing. A tiny, seventy-eight-year-old woman with a blonde ponytail and wearing a black body stocking. When she did her stretches the years just fell away; you could almost see the decades evaporating, she was that agile. "This is your time," she told the twenty or so shivering women lying on mats around her. She had such a soothing voice I almost hated to give her up.

"Everyone just quietly go at your own pace," she would whisper while smoothly executing a posterior stretch. The rest of us following her lead, grunting, heaving.

Next door in the gym there was always a badminton game in progress with much laughing, cheering. Despite my determination to experience "calm," I always wanted to join in the game; I wanted to run and lunge for a badminton bird; I wanted to score points, sweat dripping off my nose.

Outside the yoga room we could hear traffic sounds, sirens, often heavy rain. "Just leave the world behind," Betty told us. "Breathing deeply is the best tranquilizer." While a woman two mats over snored.

After my last session, someone in the class approached me. "Was that you beside me who was so good?"

I was just getting ready to preen and expose my unenlightened ego — I'm good at yoga! — when she corrected herself. "Oh no, it wasn't you. I see you're wearing black socks. It was someone in white socks." And she wandered off, perhaps deeply disillusioned.

So I've put in my time with the New Spiritualists. I've tried — dutifully — to temper my anxious Western ways with yoga classes and with infusions of New Spiritualist thinking; there's a number of books resting (for the time being) in the bookcase — they all have the words "soul," "spirit" or "life" somewhere in their titles. I've read these books, some several times, and tried to take the advice they offer. "Instead of uselessly wringing your hands in fear and dread," they all seem to be saying, "why not relax with the emotion, walk around in it, try to discover how truly wonderful the moment can be?"

I've tried this. And where I end up is where I always

end up, with or without the help of the New Spiritualists: at the dump. And then, yes, I may be lost to the
moment, but it's often not the wonderful, ecstatic, life-
enhancing moment the New Spiritualists seem to have
in mind. Because down at the dump there's a lot of garbage, nasty, smelly garbage, and hardly any of it's wonderful. Interesting, maybe. Like many of the people who
hang out there, too.

Nana, my mother-in-law, for one. Now that I've shed
my New Spiritualist ways and allowed my true worrywart
nature to blossom, Nana and I have become dumpster
pals. She's a master of the art, an expert agonizer, although she calls it "worrying." "I worry all day long, from
the moment I wake up until my head hits the pillow,"
she tells me with great satisfaction. "I worry in my sleep!"
At eighty-one, she's living proof that stress doesn't kill,
that it may, in fact, be life sustaining.

When I have tea with Nana it's actually exciting. It's
like we're having an illicit affair — the sneakiness, the
private relish — because finally we get to talk. About all
the horrible things that can happen to a person in this
life and often do. We cover everything; nothing by way
of disaster or calamity is left unmentioned. All our Doom
And Gloom stories are trotted out for each other's comment and pleasure. We get to experience fear, sadness,
dread, anger, indignation — all the delicious negatives.
Our talk is apocalyptic, breathless, eternal, neither of us
shunning what's in front of our faces. She gives me all
the details: "Tumours the size of grapefruits!"; "One
minute cleaning out the fridge, the next on a slab at the
morgue!" And that terrifying phrase "Waiting for the test

results," a phrase guaranteed to fell even the most stoic amongst us.

During tea time, if no one else is around, we indulge in the age-old passion of beating our breasts, wringing our hands at the heavens. For a time we're a couple of Mother Courages run amuck. It's almost like fun. It's almost like a terrific workout.

But now and then Nana forgets herself at the Sunday dinner table and launches into a Cancer Story or a Sudden Death Story or a What If She Doesn't Get That Job story. "Not now!" I want to kick her under the table. Because her son — my husband — can't bear this talk; he physically recoils, his shoulders hunch, his face goes red then white. You can almost see his ears flattening against his head. If the story continues, he'll fling down his napkin and leave the table.

"What's the matter with him?" Nana will ask innocently.

"He doesn't like to hear about inoperable brain tumours when he's eating roast beef and mashed potatoes," I'll tell her. "He's funny that way."

One of our favourite topics is kids: hers, mine and everyone else's.

"They're a mixed blessing," Nana's fond of saying. "You never stop worrying about them, even when they're fifty-five. You just want them to be happy and safe. You want them to outlive you."

No argument there. But what this means is keeping them alive. Even when they're beyond your control, grown up and living away from you as they should be. Even when they're still with you, struggling, shaky with their emerging independence and headed down, you believe, every disastrous path known to humankind. A Herculean task.

And so it's understood: You worry — you *have* to worry — and often that's all you can do. Your worrying becomes a protective, personal antidisaster aura that you, the one who loves them beyond all measure, hurl hopelessly in their direction. It's almost like prayer.

We all do this. We hover, we bend, we agonize.

"Did I tell you about the terrible thing that happened to Kay Bradshaw?" Nana asked during one of our recent agony sessions. "The day after her husband of forty years retired, he ran off with his physiotherapist. Kay was expecting a dream vacation to Hawaii. Her bags were packed."

"No!" I shrieked ghoulishly, clapping my hands. "Tell me all about it. Start from the very beginning. And don't leave out a single thing."

And a posse of New Spiritualists threw up their hands and went solemnly on their transcending way.

PANELLIST SCHOOL

LESSON #1 — BASIC KAFKA

Recently I spent two months in Australia participating in literary festivals, giving readings and workshops and generally having the great experience of being an "international" writer. Because I was a writer from somewhere else, the festival organizers handled me with care, even if practically no one in the country had ever heard of me or my books. Maybe it wasn't star billing — maybe I had to take the shuttle bus and not a limousine to the festival sites — but what the hell: I had a certain role to play. I was part of the "international" filler contingent, along with several other international (but otherwise marginally known) writers from Singapore, New Zealand, Scotland and Malaysia doing the festival rounds that season. Our job, it seemed, was to act as literary foliage to the stars, the heavyweights from Britain and the U.S., those writers whose print runs give you nosebleeds — Martin Amis, Anne Rice.

Before the festival season started, I spent two weeks in Sydney as writer-in-residence at Macquarie University. "Don't ask," I got in the habit of saying later, when people inquired about my stay there.

Here's how it was: Because the Department of English, Linguistics and Media had never before had a writer-in-residence, because no one there had a clue about what my job was — in fact, no one other than the department secretary was actually there — I spent two weeks experiencing life as a character in a story by Kafka. Not that I was actually looking for the quintessential Kafka experience. Not that I'd come all that way — to the Southern Hemisphere, in fact — for the privilege of experiencing bewilderment, despair, confusion, hopelessness, dread and existential angst. Not at all. I could have stayed home and done that.

So my stay at Macquarie University turned into one of those unexpected-sort-of-reality things that happens to everyone now and then. Usually you whine, "I'm having one of those days!" and leave it at that. But having one of those *fourteen* days?

By day five of my tenure I gave up, attached a note to my office door ("If anyone wants the Visiting Writer-In-Residence ... who? ...") and went sightseeing.

Meanwhile, aside from the nuisance at Macquarie University, I was in Australia! Even though it was winter there, by Canadian standards the weather was spring-like — the sky clear, the air warm. Around the campus, students lounged on the grass or tossed frisbees. One Friday afternoon, outside the dining hall where I ate, a college employee roasted six pigs on electric spits for that evening's "bush dance." Students everywhere wore shorts, the heavy khaki kind that make you think: "Outback." But now and then you'd see someone in winter wear — toque, wool scarf, quilted coat — and it seemed pretend, like they were playing at having winter. It was the same at the mall near the university, where there was an indoor skating rink filled with people, many of them wearing costumes like figure skaters you'd see on TV.

At the end of my bewildering two-week stay at Macquarie University, Gabby arrived. She was to spend the next month with me travelling around Australia to the various writing festivals, writing centres and universities where I would be making appearances. Her arrival was the culmination of a year's worth of saving money — hers and ours — plus a year's worth of heated threats about missing the trip if she "screwed up," meaning if she didn't attend school or go to work or was a colossal pain in the ass to live with. At fifteen she'd been what we now affectionately call "a dissenting adolescent" — a wild girl asking only one question of life: "Where's the party!?" Three years later she'd mellowed somewhat, and I was looking forward to spending a month with her, to "getting my hands on her," to "reclaiming" her.

But only a week before she was due to leave Canada, I'd received a frantic e-mail from Gerry: "She's broken her ankle!" She'd been at one of the several farewell parties her friends were giving her and had jumped across a ditch wearing platform shoes. The ankle, it turned out, was only bruised, but even so, Gerry decided she needed a pair of flat shoes for the trip, a decision he soon regretted. "It's taken two days of shopping," he e-mailed again, exasperated.

But in the end Gabby made it to Australia.

Because her flight landed at six-thirty in the morning and there were no early buses, I spent forty dollars and took a taxi to the airport. Gabby's plane arrived on time, but it was an hour before she came through the arrival gate. I imagined her bags were being searched for drugs. I pictured her being roughly handled and refused entry into the country. Looking anxiously through my address book for the telephone number of the Canadian Consulate, I worried that the office wouldn't be open yet. I was certain my daughter was being held in the basement below the airport, crying and bereft, and that I'd need the Consulate's help in freeing her.

But she was smiling when I finally saw her. Nothing untoward had happened; she'd been held up waiting for the luggage. We caught a taxi for the return trip to the campus apartment where I'd been staying. Giving the driver the address, I told him the ride to the airport had cost forty dollars, so the ride back into town would cost no more than that.

The driver said, "That can't be. There's no way it will cost forty dollars. More like eighty."

My daughter said, "Are you calling my mother a liar?"

I looked at her. A tall girl, she was wearing jeans, sweatshirt and platform running shoes (where were the new shoes?) and held a heavy pack on her lap. Her jaw was clenched and she looked mean. She'd just made a fifteen-hour plane trip and she wasn't taking flak from anyone. My previous vision of her imprisoned at the airport vanished.

Inside the apartment, Gabby unpacked. She'd brought three illegal substances into the country: Two loaves of wholewheat bread, two ears of corn and a small container of blackberries from our bushes at home.

"A present for you from Dad," she said.

"Weren't you worried about bringing these things through customs?" I asked. There'd been stern warnings in the airport about bringing foodstuffs into Australia — fines, imprisonment.

"A little," she said. "But they didn't look through my bag." She took out her new, flat runners and showed them to me. "Gross, eh?"

"Well, at least you won't hurt your ankle again."

"You guys," she said impatiently. "Like, that was a total overreaction by Dad. Like, I'd seriously break my ankle a week before my trip to Australia? Yeah. Right."

We ate the corn and the bread and the blackberries for dinner.

LESSON #2 — EXPERT CHILDREN

Within days we were on the literary circuit. First we took a ten-hour train ride through sheep country to Melbourne. The great thing about travelling in Australia, as far as Gabby was concerned, was that the drinking age there is eighteen, her age exactly. As soon as she realized this, she phoned her friends at home. "It's awesome!"

I overheard her saying. "Like, I can go into all the bars and if anyone tries to ID me, I flash my passport and everything's cool."

She was so pleased about being "legal" that she was constantly trying to buy me drinks. "No," I'd say, attempting some on-the-spot training, "we don't drink beer at ten-thirty in the morning. We wait for lunch or dinner."

But the thing was, she relaxed. Any apprehension she might have had about travelling with me evaporated; she started enjoying herself, started to act like a young woman. Gone was the edgy teenager I'd become used to. Ditto for the disappearance of her haranguing, censoring mother. The fact that we drank beer and wine all over Australia might have had something to do with this.

Between literary appearances in Melbourne, Wollongong and Tasmania, Gabby and I visited zoos (seventy-two pictures of kangaroos, koala bears and parrots); shopped (if I ever wander through another Food Court...); saw four movies (all romantic comedies); drank countless cappuccinos (it's difficult to get regular coffee in Australia); sampled every available brand of Australian beer (several times over); and finally, in early September, stayed with my second cousin Sheila and her husband Jack in Brisbane, where I was appearing at the Brisbane Writers' Festival.

It was here, before the festival events began, that we took a daytrip on one of Brisbane's river ferries. We'd only met Jack and Sheila twice before, when they'd visited Canada. A retired, well-off couple in their early sixties, they were energetic and welcoming, eager to show us the sights of their city.

But it was not a good day for Gabby; she was in a foul mood, sullen and withdrawn — a way she'd been for much of the time during those horrible years from age thirteen to sixteen when her emotions were all over the map. It took me by surprise; I'd become used to the engaging young woman I'd been travelling with, the one who volunteered to carry my luggage, who picked the restaurants we'd eat at and always made the right choice, who pored over guidebooks and made sensible suggestions about bus routes. I took a group picture while we were waiting to board the river ferry that day, and there beside Jack and Sheila, who are smiling and looking relaxed, stands Gabby, several feet away, glowering at me for taking the picture.

"What's the matter with you?" I managed to hiss at Gabby when my cousin wasn't listening.

She looked at me angrily. "I'm so bored! Brisbane's soooo boring! It's like Disneyland — so white and clean. So germ-free. I can't stand it."

The weather in this faux Disneyland was great, though — hot, clear blue sky, the air heavy with the scent of flowering jasmine. But it made no difference. Gabby wore the look of one who's under tenuous control — part hate, part tears. Her disgust for our boring adult lives was palpable, and it's hard not to sound inane when there's someone like that in your midst judging your every move and utterance.

Without acknowledging Gabby's black mood, the rest of us carried bravely on.

Sheila: Isn't it a wonderful day!

Me: This is so pleasant, riding around on the ferry, getting off, having coffee, having lunch. Look at all the palm trees!

Jack: That development over there is called Riverside. It was built in 1991 and is a very popular place.

Sheila: Look at all the Wattle trees! They're my favourite trees. I love trees!

Jack: At one time the area along the river was used for industry. But now some of those old buildings have been made into apartments. They're pretty expensive.

Me: This is so great, seeing the city like this. What a fabulous form of public transportation!

Sheila: People are so clever. Look at that bridge. Imagine building something like that!

Jack: It's a really interesting thing, the way they make brick. It's quite a long procedure. First they ...

The topic of my first panel at the Brisbane Festival was: "I Know Funny: Do We All Laugh At The Same Things?" The panel discussions were formal affairs. Each writer was to present a ten-minute paper on the designated topic and then participate in a question-and-answer session with the audience. The writer as essayist, then as interesting conversationalist. I wondered if the panels would resemble those TV talk shows that aimed for a cultured presence, the kind with witty and bookish panellists: dapper old men in bowties, flamboyant old women in bouffant hairdos. And how were the panellists chosen? An amusing speaker with a tightlipped one? The lame with the wild?

Panel discussions at Canadian festivals are usually freewheeling, loose affairs: a group of writers sitting around yakking about writing, often half drunk, and usually pissing each other off in the most delightful and ribald way. Not so at Australian festivals. I was imagining stiff academic discussions and an aggressively intelligent, almost hostile audience. I planned to say a few words and then read something from my latest book.

An audience of two hundred people, including uniformed school boys, waited for the four-thirty panel to begin. On the panel with me were standup comic Richard Stubbs, two writers from *Good News Week*, an Australian TV show celebrated as "zany and irreverent," and feminist cartoonist Judy Horacek. Just before we took our seats on the platform, Richard Stubbs, who was acting as chair, gathered us together in a loose circle where we all said "Hep!" like football players about to sprint onto the field.

Richard Stubbs opened the proceedings and was, of course, brilliant. I remember little of what he said. But everyone laughed. He'd just published his first book, *Still Life*, a collection of comic riffs. On the cover he's dressed like the Mona Lisa and looking very much like the original. He told the audience that he didn't have a clue what made people laugh; you were either funny or you weren't, and he said this in such a way that people were wiping tears from their eyes.

I looked alarmingly at my notes on Medieval fools and postmodern dislocation and started to feel sick. This was not an audience who'd warm up to deconstruction theory.

The next panellists, writers for the TV show, were also brilliant — a kind of Laurel and Hardy pair, except they were both the goofy one. TV couldn't have typecast them any better: tall, skinny, nerdy, long-haired, bespectacled, maybe twenty-nine or thirty-one, wearing soiled T-shirts and big black boots like the characters in Zap comics. Both of them said straight off that they didn't have a clue what made people laugh. "There's no definition," one of them declared and poured water down the front of his shirt. The audience roared. One had a joke about Pablo Neruda and the business of putting poetry on the buses: "What does a Pablo Neruda bus horn sound like?" he asked the audience. "Neruuuuda. Neruuuuda." The uniformed school boys in the front row laughed their heads off.

By now my notes were soaked with perspiration. I looked about wildly for an escape route, for someone to save me, thinking: "I shouldn't be here; there's been a terrible mistake; I'm going to throw up."

Judy Horacek, next up, was even funnier than the three guys. She'd just published *Lost In Space*, a book of cartoons. She also said she didn't know what humour was, so had looked the word up in the Oxford dictionary. "Humour: Wit, comedy, drollery, fun," and so on. The audience found the list very funny.

As it was nearing my turn, I considered getting up from my chair, announcing to the audience, "I'm not funny," and walking away from the platform in a dignified manner. The other panellists had, one after the other, worked the audience into a quivering, almost hysterical state. Expectations were running high. Was everyone expecting a giant laugh orgasm by the time it was my turn? Some kind of fulfilled release? So that afterwards, during the question-and-answer period, we could all get relaxed and cozy and satisfied together and say things like, "Wasn't that good!" and "Whew! What a workout!"

What did I do? I read half a page from my notes: "The Fool was a revered and feared personage in Medieval times ..." (The audience fearing boredom.) I read something from my books. (Heh, heh.) I kept it short. (Thank gawd, bring back the comedians.)

During this session, Gabby was sitting in the audience at first, but after Richard Stubbs' performance she wandered to the grass area at the front of the tent. I watched as she and a six-foot-tall uniformed schoolboy shared a cigarette. "Ah, she's missing people her own age!" I thought from my prison at the panellist's table. Relief at the realization that there was a reason for her former moodiness competed with my mounting panic.

"He's invited me to a movie tonight," she told me later. "I'll take a taxi. I won't be late." And then, throwing me a crumb, said, "You were pretty good up there today. The other ones weren't that funny. But you should stick to giving readings, Mom. Seriously. That's where you do best."

"We should put you on a panel," I told her. "A panel of 'expert' children. A panel of writers' children."

"Yeah, that'd be cool. I could tell about all the readings you made me go to. Remember the Denman Island Poetry Festival and that nude performance guy? That was so gross the way he jumped over our chairs. What a view! They should do that here."

LESSON #3 — PERFORMING SEALS

I was feeling more confident about the Sunday morning panel, "Words That Define A Generation," because after the humour panel on Friday afternoon I'd spent most of Saturday feverishly rewriting my notes. I was prepared for anything; I had five sheets of paper and was going to read from them like an academic. "This is a difficult topic, one that is at the heart of the writer's dilemma today," I would begin, carrying through remorselessly to my closing comments about the "writer as performing seal."

I told Sheila and Jack optimistically, "You'll want to get there early, the place will be packed." The panel was to be held in the auditorium, the festival's largest venue. My relations were from the stern world of banking and business, and this was to be their first-ever literary event.

In the green room I met up with my co-panellists: Mark Davis, the chair; Sean Condon; and Michael Wilding, one of Australia's leading fiction writers and one whose work I very much admired. (At fifty-five he looked nothing like the dope-smoking, radical politico pictured on his covers — more like a Master at a private school: grey flannels, tweed jacket, soiled white shirt.) The group of us sipped water and tried to relax.

Sean Condon, the young Australian author of *Sean & Dave's Long Drive* and *Drive Thru America*, pulled at his collar and said as we were heading towards the stage, "Oh God! I feel like a piece of shit. I don't know what I'm going to say. I'm too stupid. I shouldn't be here. There's been some terrible mistake. I shouldn't be on this panel. I don't have a single thing to say." He was wild-eyed and sweating heavily.

The auditorium was half-full. Or half-empty, depending on your anxiety level. It held about fifty people, if you counted the soundman and the festival staff standing by the door. Gabby and our relatives sat midway back in the audience.

After a few introductory words from Mark Davis, it was Sean Condon's turn. He wiped his brow, shakily poured himself some water, cleared his throat, sipped his water again. "I don't know why I'm here," he began. "I'm too stupid to be on a panel. I don't know anything." The audience laughed. Particularly enthusiastic was a large group of young women in the front rows, his fans. "I've made some notes," he stammered, "on the back of this bookmark ..." And he held it up. More laughs. He continued in this vein for fifteen minutes and managed to convey to the audience that while his generation might be terminally confused, it definitely had an edge on what makes people laugh. There was loud applause when he finished.

Both Michael Wilding and I read from our prepared texts, Michael focusing on the political climate within which literature gets written, and me on postmodernism and the writer's dilemma: write and/or perform? They were competent, thoughtful presentations, but hardly a laughfest.

Sean Condon fielded most of the questions during the session afterwards. Everyone wanted to hear what he had to say: "Well, shit, I dunno ..."

Afterwards I asked Sheila, "What did you think?"

"I thought that first speaker, Sean Something, was dreadful," she said. "The way he said the 'f' word to that journalist asking that question." (Middle-aged journalist with a mock question full of indecipherable postmodern terminology to which Sean Condon answered, "In the words of my generation: fuck off." I laughed along with everyone else.) My cousin continued. "I've never heard such language in public! That journalist's very well known. He's often on the ABC, you know. And to be treated that way in public. It was awful!"

Jack beside her nodded gloomily.

"That's nothing," Gabby declared. "You should go to a Canadian reading." And she quoted her favourite line from a Sheri-D Wilson performance piece. Right there on the crowded sidewalk, in the dazzling Brisbane sunshine, she stood back and bellowed: "Don't fuck with a fuck!"

Our relatives blanched. It was too much for them. They shuddered, then hurried away for reviving cappuccinos.

At the book-signing table, Michael Wilding and I sold a book apiece. Sean Condon had a long line at his part of the table — fifteen or twenty young women, each clutching a copy of his book, eager for an autograph. Gabby was among them.

After a few minutes it was clear that Sean Condon would be the only writer this day blessed with a book-buying public. Michael Wilding, who's published thirty-five books, said, "Christ, I can't bear this. It's ritualized humiliation."

And so, in the words of our generation, we said "fuck it" and left to get a drink.

Gabby came with us. "I'll buy," said my take-charge daughter. "You guys look like you need a beer." And went into the refreshment tent.

Michael and I found a table outside on the grass and sat down beneath the black and white Bollinger umbrella. Beside us, ferry-boats sped by on the Brisbane River.

While we waited for Gabby, Michael asked me how travelling with a teenage daughter had been.

"Pretty good," I said. "But it'll be better for both of us later. In the memory of it. In the retelling."

"You mean there'll be a book?"

"Who knows?" I said.

When Gabby arrived with our drinks, she sat down and lit a cigarette. I was struck by how beautiful she looked, how sophisticated. Her blonde hair was pulled into a low bun and she was wearing sunglasses. She could have been twenty-five years old. She asked Michael, "Do you know Sean Condon?" He was holding court with a group of young women at a nearby table.

Michael said, "Vaguely."

"Could you ask him over?" she said, taking a sip of her beer. "I'd like to talk to him about his book."

Michael smiled indulgently. "So you're a fan of literature?"

Offended, Gabby replied coolly, "Of course. I mean, all my life there've been writers around. You don't have a choice." And then: "How old is he? Sean Condon."

"Twenty-five? Thirty?" Michael said, smiling.

"Hmm," Gabby continued. "Invite him over. He sounded interesting. I liked the way he talked. Normal, not all fake like most writers. And I want to ask him how he did that. Travelled around a country and then wrote about it. That'd be an awesome thing to do. Yeah. That'd be so cool."

YOU'RE YOUNG, YOU'RE DUMB
AND YOU'RE WRONG

LESLIE INVITED US TO A GIG IN VICTORIA. HE WAS INSISTENT, declaring, "You've never actually seen the band play before a live audience. You've never seen us perform."

It was one of those dreaded hyper-real moments, like when you're at the dentist with a grey rubber dam strapped on your face and you think: Everything in my life has been leading up to this one, awful, trapped moment. In this case the moment formed itself around Leslie's lovely, pouty, anxious face staring us down, demanding, "Well? Well? Are you coming to the gig?"

Judging by his accusatory tone you'd think we'd had years of failed appearances at all kinds of childhood events — the spring concerts that went on for hours, for example, with the teeth-gritting, ear-aching band performances and the fifteen modern dance routines, one after the other, all alike; with the guitar-playing teacher seizing his moment and belting out "House of the Rising Sun" before the captured audience of six hundred; with the other teacher, the "fun one," donning a spangled Elvis jumpsuit and strutting his stuff to "Jailhouse Rock."

So Gerry and I were reacting to Leslie's implication of blame. Had we let him down so badly in the past — those countless freezing mornings on the soccer field completely forgotten by him, having permanently fled from his twenty-year-old memory — that only our attendance at this gig could redeem us?

All this was a red herring, of course. Because what Gerry and I were really nervous about was going to the gig. Suddenly it seemed we'd been living in a kind of benign bubble concerning our son's endeavours. Until this invitation, everything had been hunky-dory with him; we actually felt we'd done a good job raising him and we didn't want our bubble burst with the realization that maybe things weren't really all that great — meaning that he was living in a dream world, that his passionate involvement in the band was for naught, that the band was, in fact, horribly, embarrassingly amateurish. Or, in kid parlance, that it sucked big time.

Leslie's invitation became a kind of pivotal experience for us, bringing up huge, existential questions. Such as: What if we have to tell him the truth? What if the band's performance is like all those other childhood events — the badly produced plays that ended in tears, the baseball games lost in the final seconds for a hundred different reasons?

These questions hung menacingly between Leslie, with his giddy hope, and us, with our megatonne worry that we'd have to fake enthusiasm about the band's performance, about Leslie's performance, and that no matter what, we'd have to praise his effort — as in "You were really good! Really!" As in: "Way to hit the ball!" As in: "Better luck next time!"

We'd have to say all those things that doting parents say at Little League games. Except for one game when Leslie was fourteen. We'd taken an older poet to the game with us and he was enjoying himself immensely, sitting in the drizzle, eating his hot dog, experiencing "down-home real life," as he put it, until the third inning, when he suddenly stood up and yelled viciously, "Whose kid is that? He's terrible! Take him off first base!"

Everyone in the stands went silently apoplectic, glowering at us, outraged. Because you never, never hurl the truth at Little League players. It's just not done. What about self-esteem and team play and good effort and all that? We had to shut the poet up, but it was too late. Little League etiquette had been broken, Little League spirit reviled. And the next time I did my mother's duty in the concession stand, the other mothers, polite but chilly, kept their distance: Ostracism was mine.

So we learned that you don't deliver the truth to kids until much later. But our question was: When do you get to do this? Is there a specific time and/or event — and were we faced with it now? For how many years, and against what reason and logic, do parents have to keep praising their children's efforts? Even when, in our opinion, the efforts are lousy, inept, substandard. I had a sudden terrifying thought about one of the kids at age thirty-seven: me telling them in all the warm, caring, self-esteem-boosting ways I could muster, "That's really wonderful the way you've been able to hold down a job at the bottle exchange for three weeks. Way to go! Let's hire a hall and have a celebration!"

Does the end of active parenting occur when you finally draw a line in the sand and holler at your over-supported offspring, "You're young, you're dumb and you're wrong!" about whatever it is they're being dumb and wrong about? Perhaps this is the parent's real job: reality, truth and division — as in, "me, grown-up; you, blockhead."

Then again, maybe this is the moment when you finally zip your mouth shut forever. Because you probably don't know a damned thing anyway. And who are you to declare that their idea/effort/plan stinks? Maybe you're just jealously stifling their dreams. And haven't we all been told *ad nauseum* that we have a right to follow our dreams?

So there it was, the awful dilemma brought to a boil, and it made Gerry and me wonder whether Leslie's adulthood — for good or ill — was at hand. Was it waiting in the wings like some huge, white, impatient horse that Leslie would now ride into the florid sunset?

Was this it, we wondered? *The* significant event? Was he about to declare himself grown-up by announcing, "This is who I am, this is what I do"? Just the way I had, at eighteen, when I told my father I intended be a writer and my father blanched — he actually turned pale — and said, "You'll live a life of grief." That's what he said: a life of grief. How did he know? Where'd he get his information? You'd think I'd just told him I was going to hit the streets as a hooker; he practically fainted away. And when he recovered, he asked me sadly, "Is that what you want for yourself, Marion, a life of grief?"

"A life of grief?" I shrieked, hurling sarcasm. "Oh sure, I'd love one. Show me where to sign up." His opinion stung and stalled me, though it never stopped me. And so I'm keeping this in mind with Leslie, as a kind of footnote, trying to pull my fingers out of his flesh at last. "And about bloody time," Gerry would say.

This whole business of adulthood has got me baffled. I look back on my own young life for clues, try to pin a time, an event, an insight, when adulthood happened to me, but other than declaring that I wanted to become a writer, nothing comes to mind. Not the first love affair, or the first full-time job, or the purchase of my first car, or even the first marriage. Adulthood seems to have happened in a kind of greasy slide. Then suddenly, it seemed, there were all these obligations — other people, things to look after.

So: adulthood. I do what I always do when I'm unsure — turn to books, looking for definitions and answers.

The Buddhists say that as long as we don't want to be honest and kind with ourselves, we're always going to be infants, we'll never be grown-up. The Hindus call adulthood the wish to provide maintenance to the world. Developmental psychologist Eric Erickson tells us there are eight stages of man — stage six being something called Young Adulthood, which essentially has to do with searching for Identity and Love. But it's not until stage seven that you arrive at true adulthood and the whole business of Care kicks in — care of the persons, ideas and products you've learned to value. I'm wondering about stage 6.021, which is just a hair's width past stage five, the self-absorbing adolescence stage. This is where I peg Leslie and the girls. According to Erickson's chart, it'll be a long haul, years of crisis and retrenchment, before they reach a fully ripe stage seven, which presumably is where Gerry and I are — hapless, productive worker bees, caring for the world and everything in it. Until, that is, we slide into stage eight — the final stage, Old Age, which will yield to us that prize word "wisdom," meaning "consolation prize; the end is nigh."

The *Oxford English Dictionary* gives the word "adult" the merest nod — "mature" — preferring to dwell on the derivatives, especially "adultery," which gets the most ink, and the curious word "adulterant": "thing employed in adultery" (as in: "She fondled his throbbing adulterant …").

Human biologists claim that "mature" means the completion of an organism's developmental process, and that adulthood is when the powers of body and mind are at their peak.

Leslie mentioned this very thing last Thanksgiving, fearing we'd never acknowledge his peak. We had two tables for dinner — one for adults, one for teenagers — and he said: "I'll be forty years old and you'll still be putting me at the kids' table." And what came to mind was stemming the tide. Because once we start letting them celebrate at the table with us, they'll take over — which is what, in depressing human biology terms, they're supposed to do.

I was so addled by all this that I started dreaming about definitions. It was Dr. Laura, that rabid radio-show upholder of "morals" and "family values" who came swooping nastily into my dreams. "What!" she bawled. "You let your unmarried minor children do what? Have sex, drink alcohol, stay out past their six p.m. curfew? Shame on you. You're a stoooopid woman. They'll never become adults now. They'll never learn to accept responsibility now. You deserve every second of grief that you get!"

There it is again: a life of grief.

In lieu of learned definitions I've been searching for some handy little pamphlet about adulthood that will tell me the warning signs, a discreet brochure sitting on a table at the public library or at the doctor's office. Written in large, clear, sober sentences, spelling everything out: *Emerging Adulthood: Signs & Symptoms*. With five succinct points that I can tick off.

I'd even settle for a joke list, like the one about the signs and symptoms of childhood that I found in *Oral Sadism and The Vegetarian Personality*, edited by Glenn Ellenbogen, Ph.D.

Clinical Features of Childhood

1. Congenital onset
2. Dwarfism
3. Emotional immaturity
4. Knowledge defects
5. Legume anorexia (won't eat vegetables)

My idea for the signs of emerging adulthood would be:

1. GREED. Wants what the caregivers can't or won't

provide — beer, junk food, cell phone, car. Translates into full-time job.

2. DIMINISHED BURDENISM. The skill/talent of being a burden to others gradually wanes. Begins to feed own self.

3. SHRINKAGE. Begins to seem less large — to shrink, in fact, down to human size.

4. GIFTS. Buys caregivers actual gifts for Christmas and birthdays — gifts other than homemade cards, can openers, candles from the Bargain Store, incense.

5. LOCOMOTION. Moves out.

Gerry, of course, believes that none of the above will ever happen. During one of his gloomier moods I gave him the bottle of expensive French wine I'd been saving for his birthday.

"What's all this about?" he asked, suspicious.

"I thought you could do with a lift."

"Hah!"

"I thought I'd grease the wheels. Ease the pain."

"Hah!"

"And I want to tell you about the new motto I've got: Adult Independence for the New Millennium. I'm going to print it out, attach it to the fridge door. Think of it: Everyone gone. The place to ourselves. It's a real goal. Something we can all work towards."

"It'll never happen," he said miserably. "They wouldn't understand it. They'd have to look up the word 'adult' in the dictionary. It'd be too much work for them. It would make them tired. They'd have to go back to bed. For the rest of their lives they'll be downstairs asleep. Not working. Not going to school. Sleeping."

"You're exaggerating!"

"No, I'm not. Living with them now is harder work than when they were infants keeping us awake all night. Remember teething? And fevers? And nightmares? Remember all those broken bones?"

I remembered. "One year we had a broken bone every month for seven months. Ankles, wrists, arms. I'd forgotten about that. I got to feel so at home in the emergency ward."

"Rhapsodize if you must," Gerry snorted. "But that was the Golden Age."

It goes without saying that we went to Leslie's gig.

The band — I CAN'T STAND YOU — was playing in a club in Victoria. They were the featured act, and, to our surprise, the place was packed with nineteen- to thirty-year-olds. Leslie and his bandmates had been there for a couple of hours already, setting up. He sauntered over to our table when we sat down. He was confident and relaxed, like the host of an astoundingly successful party.

"I'll get you a better table," he told us. "You can't see anything from here."

He was wearing his rock-star outfit: Gerry's leather suit from his first wedding. The suit especially made so the wearer would look like a well-dressed gunslinger from the Wild West. On Leslie's head was the leather bush hat I'd brought him from Australia.

He moved us to a table in front of the stage — telling a group of kids to shove over — and then brought us a couple of beer (*bought* us beer!). Then he excused himself, saying he had things to do. I watched him greeting people; I watched his friends from Sidney slapping him on the back. He was so relaxed I wondered if he'd taken something. But he'd often said, "I never do anything before a gig. You have to be 'on' for the music."

At ten p.m., when the band members mounted the stage, the crowd roared its approval and rushed for the dance floor. My heart was pounding when they began. I thought: "Hey, I've seen this movie before. There's all this trepidation before the performance, but the untried singer/pianist/band turns out to be great … just fine."

As was our son's band. "Thank fucking Christ," whispered Gerry.

"Mock pop," they called their sound, very tight musically, a crowd pleaser. During the set I was surprised to see my normally reserved husband threading his way through the dancers taking pictures, at one point even standing on a chair to get a good stage shot. He'd never bothered taking pictures of the sixteen spring concerts we'd attended over the years.

Between sets, Leslie's beefy friend from Sidney, the valedictorian when they'd graduated from high school, leaned over and said to Gerry, "It's so cool he's got your support. My folks are like that, too. My dream is to become a wrestler for the World Wrestling Federation. I'm going east next week for training and my parents are behind me one hundred percent. You can't do nothing without support."

"Right," Gerry said, looking at me. I knew what he was thinking: "Leslie's not stupid. Now that he's shown us how good his band is, now that he has our genuine approval, he'll be living at home forever."

My favourite comment about adulthood has to be the one I overheard on an evening walk. I passed by a neighbour shovelling dirt into a wheelbarrow while his sweatshirt-hooded teenage son looked on. The man paused in his labours to deliver a Lesson For Life. "Always remember one thing, son," he said to the boy, who was wearing a foot cast. "Not all adults have high IQs."

RITARDANDO

IT WAS ANOTHER FAMILY EVENT, ONE OF THOSE HUGE
birthday dinners — Nana's eighty-second — that everyone knocks themselves out for. Fifteen people gathered at our house to eat and drink and hoot it up, and
before the night was out sing "Happy Birthday" at least
a dozen times. Gerry's stylish sisters, Karen and Ellen,
and their husbands had flown in from Toronto and
Calgary. It's always great when the sisters visit because
as soon as they arrive they buy groceries in feast-like
quantities, the kind of things we never have on a regular
basis, like three dozen New York strip steaks, and barbecue chickens, and all kinds of snack foods, cheeses,
chips, rice crackers, exotic fruits. And ingredients for
the latest fabulous dessert circulating the parties in Toronto and Calgary — the dessert that will be the main
event at this birthday dinner: a delicate chocolate mousse
pie with slabs of homemade chocolate meringue for the
crust.

And then they buy wine — not two or three bottles,
carefully chosen with pursed lips and clenched purses,
but an entire flamboyant case of vintage French

Bordeaux. Plus several flats of beer, a selection of after-dinner liqueurs and large-sized bottles of gin, vodka, rye and scotch because Nana likes a *real* drink now and then.

"What do you want?" they ask, driving off in their rented car, a Lincoln or a Lexus. "Can we bring you anything back?"

And Gerry always says, "Yeah, bring me a fleet of dancing girls." And one time his sisters did that, too, only it was them doing the dancing in their bikini underpants with red and blue balloons attached to their bras — the after-dinner show — and Karen's husband Gord ran around with the fork from his Swiss army knife trying to pop the balloons, only it didn't work — the points were too dull.

So off they go shopping while I, the visited sister-in-law, the live-in daughter-in-law, get to sit in the best, cozy living-room chair and read because everything is wonderful, there's nothing I can do other than make sure the toilets are clean and there are enough towels in the bathrooms, and ironed napkins for the birthday dinner, and cans of mixer in the fridge.

And it's also great to realize we'll be eating off the food they buy for a week after they've left. I'm happy about not spending money. That's one of my greatest pleasures, not spending money — not spending money I don't have, I mean. Because whenever I get a larger amount than normal, it's gone fast in several huge gestures and then I'm back to studying the family finance book, the place where the many debits and few credits are entered, studying it like it was some holy book filled with secret messages about how to squeeze hope out of overdrawn accounts.

So the guests have arrived and gone off shopping. And they're laughing as they pull out of the driveway, rolling down the car window, waving goodbye. Those women are always laughing. Everyone's looking forward to sampling their latest hot hors d'oeuvre when they return. I'm certain the sisters will have a new recipe for us to try. Last visit it was water chestnuts wrapped in bacon and broiled with a barbecue sauce.

Ellen's husband Wallace, whom everyone agrees is the family eccentric, has driven off with them, too. He's been put in the back seat and grins at us like a chauffeured movie star, something he's told us he wouldn't mind being. "I wouldn't object to fame," he says, seriously, every time he visits. "I wouldn't object at all."

Wallace won't be going grocery shopping, though. He'll be prowling the local stores for flowers for the table — and they must be certain flowers: Bird-of-paradise and calla lilies and tiger lilies — plus a special kind of greenery that's hard to find. But the big thing, the most important thing, is that porous green substance called Oasis that you buy from the florist. It's like a stiff sponge that you stick the flowers into, and Wallace says he must have some, he simply must, or his decorations will be ruined.

Returning later, the sisters are still laughing and the car trunk's full of food. The rest of us help carry the bags inside, and who says it's not like Christmas? Because there are extra things, like three-foot-long baguettes and Gerry's favourite dill pickles, Strubbs, a pickle that's hard to find on the coast, and peameal bacon, another thing he loves; there's a bag full of deli meat, cocktail onions, Portuguese buns. And Wallace is clutching several bouquets of paper-wrapped flowers with such importance you'd think we were having a wedding.

The kids help, too, with the unloading, going directly for the flats of beer and giving each other significant looks. They're eighteen, nineteen and twenty-one now, but last year we lumped them all together and declared them grown-up. "We've absolutely had enough," we said. "We're sick of power struggles and worrying about things that are *your* business, like are you going to graduate? And are you going to keep that job? Pay your bills? Stay clean and healthy?" Puffing ourselves up, we said, "WE'RE DECLARING YOU ADULTS! And we're going to treat you that way, too. Just don't mess up or, like adults, you'll be looking for another cave to dwell in."

"Cool," they said.

And so far so good.

When the relatives visit, the kids think they're in some kind of movie about opulence and good times. They think they're in suspended gratification because of the giving that goes on — food, drink, presents, interest. And it's hard for them to resist, hard to act like jerks when everyone thinks they're so incredibly great. Helping unload those flats of beer, they're no doubt trying to figure out how to scoff a six-pack or two so their friends can come over later, when the birthday party's well underway, and take a lesson with them in how to live really well, how to revel in times of plenty. Why else have these birthday celebrations or Christmases or Easters or anniversaries or any other good-news event if not to do that? And these kids, these exuberant learners, are finding out what motions go into making the good times happen, and that's important, too, because we want them learning the right motions and understanding about balance. What is family solidarity, family closeness, if not the bunch of you speaking the same language, embracing life with similar motions and realizing where you're slightly different and knowing that's okay, too, somehow you always fit in.

Take Leslie and our weekend trip to Calgary last fall for Ellen's birthday. Ellen didn't know we were coming. Karen was there, too, having flown in from Toronto, and so was "Uncle" Jimmy from Pender Island, the family's last visible hippie — beard, grey ponytail, crumpled clothes — and the oldest of Nana's four kids. Everyone calls him "Uncle," even Nana, and we think this has something to do with his long beard, the perceived aura of wisdom gleaned from his heyday years in the 1960s.

The first night there, Uncle Jimmy and his girlfriend asked Leslie if he wanted to walk to the corner store for smokes and Leslie said, "Yeah!" feeling honoured at being asked. As soon as they left the house, Uncle Jimmy lit up a joint and handed it to Leslie, and Leslie was in a panic because he doesn't like smoking weed — he says it gives him anxiety attacks. But what do you do? he later asked. When it's your own well-loved, good-natured uncle treating you like an equal, finally treating you like a man? The uncle turning on his heel towards his nephew — long and skinny like him; they could be doubles — with the joint outstretched and choking out the word, " 'Ere."

"You take a very small puff for form's sake," Leslie said, "because you don't want to offend your uncle, and you hope the stuff doesn't take."

But now it's Nana's birthday and the party's roaring along; it's well into the night, because when Gerry's sisters lay on a meal it never begins before eight. And it must be ten or eleven, during that messy stretch between dinner and dessert, when things heat up. All three leaves for our dining-room table have been used and fifteen people are squeezed around it, "boy, girl, boy, girl" as Wallace insisted, but there were more girls than boys and he was piqued for a moment about that because it made the look unbalanced. His flower arrangement is lovely, though — a long, narrow display of lilies, orchids, greenery and bird-of-paradise extending the length of the table like a floral divide.

Several bottles of wine have been emptied and Wallace is doling out small gifts for the "ladies," and our girls, Gabby and Lee, resplendent in patchy Blondisima hair and nose studs, are beaming while opening their gifts — tiny acorns dipped in gold. Never before have they been treated so regally, with such hovering care.

Looking around the table, that old joke suddenly hits me, the one that goes like this: "It's a tradition in our family. Every woman's hair turns blonde at forty." Because it was blondes to the left of me, blondes to the right. Even Nana is technically blonde. She has dazzling white hair with a name: Platinum Allure from Clairol, like our Blondisima girls. And the rest of us, too. Gerry's sisters: Karen with blonde streaks and Ellen, whom everyone calls "old dependable," a reddish blonde; my own twin sisters, Marilyn and Pats, with blonde-tipped pixie cuts; and me, a natural blonde thanks to Sun-In spray-in hair lightener. Even Mutz, our dog, lying nearby hoping for scraps, is a blonde retriever.

All these Clairol blondes at one table — it made you think Swedish: everyone transformed into a long-limbed beauty, everyone languidly sexual. I said this out loud and Wallace hooted, "What about me? I belong to Clairol, too!" and Gerry shouted, "So do I!"

It was true.

There I was, returning from Australia after a two-month book tour, and I was picked up at the airport by a man with dark blonde hair — my husband. When I left on the trip he was silvery grey but during my absence he had succumbed like the rest of us and, in a reckless youth-grabbing gesture, had dyed his hair.

"I can't tell whether I'm an old guy in need of a facelift or a young guy who looks really bagged," he's said several times since.

And he's still a dark blonde and the jury's still out.

Nana's seated at the head of the birthday table, wearing a long white caftan. Her huge imitation-gold crucifix, the one that must weigh twelve pounds and that we call her armour, hangs off her neck. There's nothing faint about the effect; it's strictly biblical in the face of so much unholy hilarity. Not that she's a pious observer by any stretch. "Just so you don't forget Who's in charge," she says, patting her necklace and downing another glass of wine. And we're not sure if she means herself or that Other Guy — the Big Boy in the sky, the One she's convinced puts in overtime looking after the rest of us, too.

Nana's birthday presents are heaped before her and while she's opening them Karen tells a story. Of how Toronto friends paid fourteen hundred dollars for a Chihuahua puppy so small he could fit in the palm of your hand, a small shivery puppy called Juan. They'd had the puppy for two weeks when they went out one Saturday night for dinner, and when they returned home they discovered that their cat Noodles had eaten the dog. All that was left was Juan's tiny leg lying on the living-room rug. There was no trace of the dog, no blood or anything to indicate that he'd met his grizzly end, because the cat had done a really professional job.

"Good thing they found the leg," Karen said, "otherwise they'd be going crazy calling and calling and searching everywhere for Juan and not finding him and having sleepless nights thinking he might be lost somewhere in the house and eventually starving to death in a gruesome way."

Uncle Jimmy said, "Well, all is not lost. At least now they'll be getting a three-legged stool in the cat box."

And everyone howled at the wit, but after the laughs died down the topic changed. Being a writer, I tried to ask questions; I wanted details. But by now everyone was grabbed by Wallace's announcement that a wonderful new food discovery had been made. And it turned out this discovery was a Tomato and Onion Sandwich — but not any tomato and onion sandwich; no, this one is special because the onions have to be Walla Walla onions and you can only get them at certain times of the year.

Wallace divulged that he'd recently spent an entire week scouring Washington State looking for these very onions. He finally found some at a farm stand outside, of all places, Walla Walla, Washington. And he brought as many as he could across the border, but they don't keep long in the fridge, so he only had enough onions for three or four weeks of tomato and onion sandwiches.

"Enough about onions!" Gerry suddenly yelled, and cranked up the stereo. "Time to dance!"

In a flash Karen and Ellen had kicked off their shoes and were on the carpet singing along to "Staying Alive," doing all the John Travolta moves — *Ah, ah, ah, ah, staying aliiiiiive* … They're both tone-deaf, can't sing a note, but this has never stopped them.

Soon everyone else was dancing, too. Even Nana, tossing her arthritis aside; even Wallace with his chronic lack of rhythm, jerking about the living room like a rapidly deflating balloon. And Gerry, whom Nana says could charm the balls off a brass monkey, was at his charming best, jiving expertly with my twin sisters — one in either hand — and spinning them around like the pair of identical tops they are. And Gabby and Lee with their minimalist moves, all cool and taut but in perfect post-Travolta time, enticed a pair of shy uncles

— the twins' husbands — onto the carpet to dance. Uncle Jimmy, in his way, too, was dancing. He was seated on the living-room couch, his forty-five-year-old girl-friend nestled on his lap, her denim miniskirt bunched at the top of her thick thighs. The pair of them were grinning serenely, nodding their heads to the music. And sitting cross-legged on the floor beside his uncle was Leslie, looking like a skinny monk doing time before his Buddha.

Before I left the table to join the dancers, I paused. This halting was a "sacred ritardando," a way of being present in the midst of things, a way of both participating in and absorbing the scene before me. Ritardando is a musical term meaning "becoming gradually slower." But I like to think of it as the pause between moments.

It was a long pause this evening because I was still filled with questions about the unlucky Juan. I couldn't stop myself; I just had to know more. Even though I'd laughed along with everyone else when I heard the story about a cat eating a dog. About a leg not much bigger than a toothpick lying on the living-room rug. About fools who pay fourteen hundred dollars for a dog. About the almost universal revulsion for Chihuahuas except, perhaps, in Mexico, where nubile señoritas keep them hidden beneath their shawls, safe against their damp breasts, and where cats frequently turn up as entrées, served to unsuspecting tourists fanning themselves in the heat with their guidebooks and believing they're eating authentic Mexican cuisine, which, as it turns out, they probably are. Tourists happy to grab a decent meal before taking the rented car to see the sights at Ixtapalapa. And then scouring the Mexican countryside for interesting shapshots, stopping at a roadside shanty, perhaps, and discovering poor people; and there, amidst the observed squalor, finding a litter of Chihuahua puppies squirming in the dirt like large pink maggots.

And did a certain Toronto couple hand over fourteen hundred dollars then and there for a puppy that remained hidden in the man's pocket for the return trip home? And is there a family in Mexico, no longer poor — that fourteen hundred dollars like a lottery win to them and all their relatives? And are they now hooting it up at *their* Grandma's birthday celebration because they finally have the necessary funds to likewise be smuggled into the great U.S. of A.?

And it seems there's no end to this, or to any of our stories.

M.A.C. Farrant is the award-winning author of *What's True, Darling* (Polestar, 1997), *Altered Statements* (Arsenal Pulp, 1995), *Raw Material* (Arsenal Pulp, 1993) and *Sick Pigeon* (Thistledown, 1991). Her work has been dramatized for television and radio, and appears regularly in magazines such as *Adbusters* and *Geist*. She is also a contributor to the anthologies *Concrete Forest: Canadian Urban Fiction* (McClelland and Stewart, 1998) and *Tesseracts 7* (Tesseract Books, 1998). M.A.C. Farrant lives in Sidney, British Columbia, where she is co-producer of the popular Sidney Reading Series.

POLESTAR BOOK PUBLISHERS take pride in creating books that introduce discriminating readers to exciting writers. These independent voices illuminate our lives and engage our imaginations.

Pluto Rising: A Katy Klein Mystery • *by Karen Irving*
The first in a series of gripping mysteries featuring Katy Klein, a smart, down-to-earth female sleuth. This mystery has a unique twist, though: Katy's profession as an astrologer helps her uncover valuable clues.
1-896095-95-X • $9.95 CAN / $8.95 USA

Pool-Hopping and Other Stories • *by Anne Fleming*
The characters in *Pool-Hoopping* come from different generations and diverse backgrounds, but all sense disorder rippling beneath the fragile surface of existence. This compels them to act in curious ways. Witty and engaging stories by a superb new writer.
1-896095-18-6 • $16.95 CAN / $13.95 USA

West by Northwest: British Columbia Short Stories
by David Stouck and Myler Wilkinson, eds.
A brilliant collection of short fiction that celebrates the unique landscape and literary culture of BC. Includes stories by Bill Reid, Ethel Wilson, Emily Carr, Wayson Choy, George Bowering, Evelyn Lau, Shani Mootoo and others.
1-896095-41-0 • $18.95 CAN / $16.95 USA

Comfort Zones • *by Pamela Donoghue*
"There is that unmistakeable tang of the real which comes with attention to the textures of experience — an attention so close we might call it love." — Don McKay
1-896095-24-0 • $16.95 CAN / $13.95 USA

Sitting in the Club Car Drinking Rum and Karma Kola: A Manual of Etiquette for Ladies Crossing Canada by Train
by Paulette Jiles
This elegant, quirky work of detective fiction has become a cult classic. Special 10th Anniversary edition.
0-919591-13-2 • $12.95 CAN / $10.95 USA